Devoted Reality

A Novel by
E. Nigma

To submit a manuscript for our review, email us at submissions@majorkeypublishing.com

Acknowledgment/Dedications – N/A

Author Notes – N/A

Contact/Social Media Info

Facebook - www.enigmakidd.com
IG - enigmakidd
Snapchat - ericnigma
Twitter - @NigmaEric
Email - enigmakidd@gmail.com

Chapter 1

The Affair

In a local cell phone shop located in a suburban area of Dallas, it's closing time as several workers are making their way out of the store after a long day. As always, two workers remain behind to close and clean the store, prepping for the next day. Tonight's workers are Chris and Tracy, who are exhausted themselves but have a long night ahead of them. It's Friday, which means it was stock day. All the items delivered earlier had to be cataloged and checked into their system, in addition to the cleaning that needed to be done. As Chris locks the front door behind his exiting coworkers, there's a look of frustration in his eyes. It seemed like he and Tracy, the only two black employees in the shop, are constantly chosen for closing on stock days. Tracy has already pulled out the inventory and is already logging the items into the computer when Chris makes his way over.

"Doesn't this shit just piss you off?" He says as he looks over several boxes that have been pulled out. "I mean, it seems like every time there's a big shipment, me and you are stuck stocking through the night. I mean, when was the last time someone other than us had to do this shit?"

Tracy chuckles as she enters an item into the system. She agrees with her coworker that the supervisor seems to choose them more than others. The two have become really close throughout the year and a half they have been working together. While she agreed that they were always getting screwed over with the stocking duties, she didn't mind it much because it allows her to spend a little extra time with her friend. This time, however, is different. Tracy needs to break some news to Chris but was struggling to do it. She sighs as she decides it's time to let him in on her secret.

"Hey, so, um... I got something to tell you," she says before letting her hair down, removing her scrunchie, and making sure it was presentable. "I didn't tell anyone else this, but today's gonna be my last day."

Chris is stunned as he stops what he's doing and walks over to his friend.

"Last day? Are you serious?" He asks. "I mean, you didn't give notice or anything?"

"I was, but I was notified this morning about it a job out in Houston," Tracy explains. "They want me to start on Monday, which is a quick turnaround, I know, but it's something I can finally use my degree for. Besides, Templeton is a dick, and I didn't feel like talking to him anyway. I'm just gonna leave a note for him to see when he comes in Monday. Oh my God, if you're here Monday when he gets in, please watch for the look on his face. If you can, snap a photo and send it to me. I would love to see it."

Chris chuckles as he's still struggling to take everything in. The move is so sudden, and he can't believe Tracy had been keeping this from him.

"Houston, huh?" He replies as he begins helping out with the inventory. "So, what's your husband gonna do?"

"Well, for now, he's gonna stay behind and get things together here. We're gonna have to put our things in storage until we're ready to officially move," Tracy answers. "There's a branch of the company he works for out there too, so he's in the process of being transferred. I'll be looking for apartments while I'm down there, but for now, I'll be in a hotel."

Chris nods his head with understanding.

"Wow. I mean... that's a big move so quickly. I'm... I'm happy for you," he says, trying to remain positive even though he's hurting a little bit knowing he's losing his friend. "I'm not gonna lie, I'm gonna miss having you around here. You made this shit bearable, you know."

"Yeah. Truth is I wouldn't have never lasted here if it wasn't for you," Tracy replies, sharing her friend's sentiments. "I remember when I first started here, you were the only one who took me under your wing and helped me get my sales skills on point. I would have never made quota if it wasn't for you."

"Bullshit, you were a natural," Chris replies. "You just needed the technical knowledge. Your sales skills were already on point."

"I see someone has forgotten them few months where I averaged only two phones for the month," Tracy replies with a smile. "Templeton was about to write me up until you jumped in and saved me like a knight in shining armor. I never did thank you for that. You can say what you want, but me and James were struggling back then, and I really needed this job to work out. I couldn't have done it without you. Thanks."

Chris smiles as he nods his head.

"Yeah, I was being nice then. I thought you were cute, and anytime I could spend with someone fine, I tend to take full advantage of it," Chris admits, causing Tracy to look up from her computer towards him.

"Oh, so you thought I was cute?" She replies with a smirk.

"Yeah, I did, but that was before I was officially married," Chris points out. "I was still in the single mind frame even though me and Alexis were together. Was still testing the waters, so to speak just to make sure I wasn't making a mistake. Was sick as shit when I found out you were married though. Alas, what could have been."

Tracy starts laughing as she gets back to work on her computer. From their past conversations, she knew Chris had a thing for light-skinned women, and his wife, Alexis, seemed like the perfect woman for him as she met all his standards. When she attended the wedding almost a year ago, she felt a little strange seeing her friend getting married. She didn't think Chris was attracted to her, but to hear him admit that she was cute was stunning, to say the least. She was the exact opposite of his wife, being dark-skinned, shorter, and more reserved. Tracy wasn't as glamourous as his wife as well, as she tends to keep her look basic. Other than her hair, which was her only vice as it has to be on point at all times, even while working. Alexis, however, was glamourous from head to toe, keeping with the latest styles and trends. So to hear Chris's thoughts about her being cute brought an itch she's been wanting to scratch ever since the two became close. She decides it was time to scratch that itch.

"Hey, Chris. Since this is the last time I'm gonna see you, I have a confession to make," she says, looking towards her friend. "I... well, when we first met way back when I actually was a little attracted to you as well."

"Really?" A curious Chris responds.

"Yeah. I mean, it's a little embarrassing, but I thought you were kinda cute too," Tracy admits, getting her true feelings out for the first time. "I mean, I always thought highly of you, and once we became cool and I got to know you, all those thoughts were what they were. I never saw myself being as close to someone like you, especially while being married. I guess what I'm trying to say is I took a few glances of you too when we first met."

A confident Chris nods his head with a big smile on his face.

"See, I knew it," he boasts as Tracy rolls her eyes. "I knew you had a thing for me. I felt that shit from day one."

"Negro, please. Your ass didn't know shit," Tracy fires back. "Like I said, I thought you were cute when we first met. Knowing you like I do now, I can't believe I even entertained the thought."

"Oh, so you entertained thoughts?" Chris replies, making his way over towards his friend. "See, your story keeps changing more and more. I think you liked me a little more than you're letting on."

"Come on, Chris. We got a lotta work to do, so can we get it together?" Tracy responds, going back to her computer.

"Not 'til you admit the truth," Chris replies as he towers over her. "Admit it, you wanted to be a little more than friends when we first met."

"I'm not about to entertain your ass," Tracy replies, working on her computer. "Now, come on, let's finish this."

Chris chuckles as he quickly reaches down and brushes his finger on Tracy's ear, causing her to yelp and jump up.

"Chris! Don't do that!" She exclaims while giggling.

"Then admit to me that you wanted to be a little more than friends," Chris replies as he continues to approach his friend.

Tracy is giggling as she's backed into a corner with nowhere to run. Chris reaches for her ear again but is blocked off by Tracy this time, who grabs his wrists. The two are playfully wrestling with each other when Chris gains control of her, pinning her to the wall with her arms over her head. The laughter between the two slowly fades as they get a glimpse of each other's eyes. Chris peers into Tracy's dark brown eyes as if he's pulled in by her beauty. While Tracy has a hard time looking away from Chris's light brown eyes. His muscular build always attracts Tracy, and to be this close to him was more than she could have hoped for. He always has the perfect cologne that intoxicates her daily. With that fragrance, combined with his freshly cut fade and perfect smile, she found herself yearning for his affection. The tension between them is thick as neither one of the friends knows what to say next. With their attraction to each other at its peak, the friends don't know how to react. As Chris moves in to kiss Tracy, she turns her head, denying him a chance.

"We... we better get back to work," she replies quietly.

Chris slowly nods his head before releasing his grasp on Tracy's wrists. She quickly walks back towards her computer and begins working as Chris takes a deep breath before continuing his work as well.

About forty minutes have passed as both Chris and Tracy are in the back storeroom putting away the now logged inventory. Tracy is struggling to put a box on the top shelf when Chris looks and notices her body fully extended. He snaps out of his glance and quickly makes his way over behind her, helping her balance the box to put it in its place. His body pressed upon hers for a brief moment, excites her slightly. She hasn't felt the touch of a man for a couple of months now since she and her husband weren't as intimate as they once were. She thinks about the playfulness between her and Chris earlier and realizes that's the most she's felt a man touch her in a long while. As the box is quickly set on the top shelf, Tracy turns to Chris as they glance into each other's eyes once more. Chris can tell she's a little uneasy.

"My bad. I was trying to get the box-"

"No, no, it's okay. It's fine," Tracy responds, reassuring her friend. "Thanks for the help."

Tracy quickly walks off, taking a seat in a nearby desk, looking over some paperwork. Chris continues to sort through the inventory as the two take subtle glances at each other off and on. As he finishes up, he looks over things before turning his attention back towards Tracy.

"Looks like we're good to go," he says as he approaches her.

"Yeah. Paperwork is straight," Tracy says as she rises from the desk area.

They both try to speak at the same time before laughing nervously.

"My bad, go ahead," Chris says.

"No, you go first. I'm sorry," Tracy replies.

"Please, Trace, I insist," Chris responds, awaiting her words.

There is an awkward silence between the two before Tracy decides to try to speak her mind.

"Well... I guess I wanna say thank you again," she responds, holding back her true feelings. "I... um... I guess that's all I wanted to say. Thank you."

Chris nods his head as Tracy walks over and hugs him. He takes in her very essence as the scent of perfume pulls at him. They once again make eye contact as the touch of their bodies brings something out of both friends. Once again, they are at the brink of kissing when Chris' cell phone interrupts the mood.

Tracy backs away to allow him to answer. Chris takes his phone out of his pocket and notices his wife calling him before quickly answering the line.

"Hey, baby... No, I'm still at the job," he says to his wife. "No... I'll be home in a few... yeah... okay... love you too... bye."

Chris hangs up the phone and looks back at Tracy.

"Hey, Trace. Look... I'm-"

"No worries," Tracy responds, cutting off her friend. "It... it was a moment of weakness on both our parts. No need to talk about it, or whatever."

Chris nods his head in agreeance.

"Yeah, I guess it was," he agrees.

"I mean, seriously, what were we thinking?" Tracy says with a chuckle. "I mean, we're both married. How much sense would that make?"

"True, true," Chris replies, nodding his head.

"Could you imagine what would happen if we did something like that?" Tracy says with a nervous laugh. "I mean, how could we live with yourselves?"

"So true," Chris replies before pausing a moment. "Of course, if we did act on it, and do our thing, nobody would know. It could be destiny."

Tracy's nervous laugh begins to fade as she starts to entertain the idea of hooking up with her friend.

"Right, but again, I think we did the right thing," she says. "Technically, you're right, nobody will know what we did... well, wouldn't know had we done it. Not to mention that we won't see each other after tonight so we won't ever have to live with it. It would literally be impossible for anyone to find out and... aw the hell with it!"

Tracy has had enough trying to fight her feelings as she moves in and aggressively begins kissing her longtime friend, much to his surprise. Chris reacts as he begins feeling on her breasts, which drives Tracy wild. She quickly begins to un-buckle his belt and starts undressing him. Chris returns the favor as he quickly pulls her shirt off between kisses and starts to take off her pants as she kicks off her shoes. Tracy pushes Chris to the storeroom floor as the coldness of the floor sends chills down his spine. Tracy chuckles as she notices his re-action.

"You didn't think I was gonna go on that cold, nasty ass floor, did you?" She mocks as she mounts him.

Chris is about to respond but is silent as Tracy grabs his shaft and inserts his manhood inside of her. The feeling of Chris inside of her causes instant bliss. Not only is this the first touch from a man in months, but it's her fantasy coming true, proving that she was into Chris more than what she led him to believe. She slowly starts grinding on her friend making sure he felt every pump of her body on him. Chris closes his eyes as Tracy's grind gets him harder than he has been for a while. Unlike Tracy, Chris and his wife have sex regularly, but he finds himself bored with her antics at times. She wasn't into trying new things, and while the sex was good with his wife, he has grown tiresome of the same old thing day in and day out. To feel something new is a pleasure for him, and the fact that it was Tracy made the pas-sion feel even better. She lets out several moans as she increases her grind on her friend. Tracy wanted this to last as long as she could. The feelings she felt were rushing throughout her body as a smile enters her face. Chris decides to turn the tables on his friend as he quickly turns her over towards the ground sending the coldness rushing through her body.

"What's that about you not being on this cold, nasty

floor?" He mocks, causing Tracy to giggle.

Chris begins putting in work as he grinds on Tracy, much to her delight. With each thrust comes louder moans from Tracy, who allows Chris to take over her entire body. The passion is driving her wild as she moans louder and louder before trying to fight back a bit. She didn't want to pique too quickly. She didn't want it to stop. His touch as he ran his fingers up and down her body felt so good to her. Once he started fondling her breasts while stroking her, Tracy begins wavering as her body becomes weak. Chris' stroke was magnificent with perfect rhythm; unlike anything she's felt before. Her husband wasn't into pleasing her the few times they would have sex. It was more about him and getting his, but Tracy can tell the sex session she's currently experiencing wasn't about Chris. He was taking his time making sure she was taken care of as well, which excites her even more. Chris is looking to test her will as he lifts one of her legs up, continuing to grind her with passion. Tracy finally breaks as the position she's in has her too weak to fight off the pleasure any longer. She fills the room with moans as she has her first orgasm in quite some time. Chris, knowing he's broken her down, moans slightly as well as he finishes up himself. Tracy opens her eyes and watches Chris's muscular body tensing up just as he finishes his orgasm before collapsing on top of her. Both friends, now lovers, are out of breath as they gaze into each other's eyes once again. Tracy clinches him tightly, not wanting him to come out of her just yet. After several moments Chris rolls over to the side of her, finally breaking their connection. He chuckles as he watches Tracy cover her face with embarrassment.

"This was nice," Chris says, finally breaking the silence.

"Just nice?" Tracy replies, looking towards him.

"Maybe a little more than nice," Chris responds with a chuckle.

Tracy leans in and kisses Chris once more before backing away with a sigh.

"So, what now?" Chris asks.

"What now is we go our separate ways," Tracy answers.

"Do we have to really do that?" Chris inquires. "Look, Tracy, I-"

"Chris, don't," Tracy says, cutting off her friend. "I didn't look to do this, you know. I wasn't trying to get one off before I left. What happened, happened. It was a one-time thing, and we're gonna leave it at that."

Chris nods his head as both he and Tracy begin getting dressed.

"The store is ready for closing, but I suggest we leave the door open to air out a little," Tracy suggests.

Chris nods his head with agreeance as Tracy makes her way out of the storage room back into the main floor. Chris sighs with his feelings running wild.

About fifteen minutes later, the two friends are getting their things together as Chris locks up the inventory room. He looks around the area making sure everything is taken care of before glancing at Tracy.

"I guess this is it," he says, breaking the silence.

"Yeah, it is," Tracy says. "I gotta say, I never thought I'd actually feel sad about leaving this place."

"Well, after what we did, I would hope it would be a little harder for you to go," Chris quips, causing Tracy to smile.

"It definitely will be something that will be on my mind for a long while," Tracy responds before walking up to her friend and sharing a quick kiss. "Take care, Chris."

"You too," Chris responds.

They look at each other once more before Tracy walks out of the store for the last time. Chris follows her as he sets the alarm before making his way out as well. After exiting the store, he locks the door and turns his attention toward Tracy. He watches as she enters her car and drives off, waving at him in the process. He waves back, sighing, knowing that this would be the last time he would ever see her in person. *Sure they can keep in touch via social media, but this would be the last time he'd smell her perfume or have playful fights with her,* he thinks. It was as if she was walking out of his life forever, and after the lovemaking session, they just had it would be hard not to have her around. After sorting through his thoughts, Chris makes his way to his car and pulls off with Tracy still fresh in his mind.

Chapter 2

Team Experiment

A little over two years have gone by since Chris and Tracy's secret affair. With a higher paying job came more responsibilities, Tracy learns. She's in her apartment working after hours going over paperwork for her early morning meeting the next day. She's in her dining room, trying to focus on the piles of work she's been assigned, but struggles to concentrate due to her husband, James, who is watching TV in the nearby living room. The couple's marriage hasn't been much better since relocating to Houston. They still struggle to connect sexually with each other. It didn't help that James has let himself go, as the once ripped abs Tracy loved on her husband have been replaced by several layers of fat. He's also developed man boobs and rarely kept his hair cut, which is an instant turn-off to her. Her job keeps her busy, so she doesn't have much time to dwell on her sexual inactivity, but every now and then, she would long for his touch even with his abundance of flaws. Even though those times were scarce, when it did come about, James was either too tired or uninterested in having sex with her leaving her unfulfilled many nights. She's trying to work on her reports when James's cackling interrupts her once more, causing frustration.

"James," she says, trying to grab her husband's attention.

He doesn't respond as his full attention is connected to the TV. He starts laughing loudly once again, causing Tracy to grab her head.

"James," she says loudly, trying to get her husband's attention to no avail.

Tracy has had enough as she gets up from the dining room and makes her way in front of the TV.

"James, I'm talking to you," she says as he tries to wave her away.

"My bad, Trace. I'm just trippin' on this show. Can you... please?" James replies as he motions her to get out of the way.

Tracy rolls her eyes in defeat as she takes a seat next to James on the couch. As she watches the show, she's confused why a reality show has her husband's attention.

"You're over here giggling like a schoolgirl watching reality TV? Are you serious right now?" Tracy asks, trying to gain an understanding.

"Sweets, this is Team Experiment. Not your run of the mill reality show," James points out with his eyes never leaving the screen. "It's reality, but it's a game show. They have all kinds of competitions and shit like that. All these folks are locked up together, and it's crazy as hell with all the drama and stuff. Can't believe you're not into this."

"Who has time for TV these days?" Tracy responds, hinting at her work. "Can't you watch this upstairs? I'm trying to get some work done, and I have an early meeting in the morning."

"Can't. TV's out again," James replies, causing Tracy to sigh.

"Again? James, why don't you just buy another TV?" she

responds. "These little fixes don't seem to be working. It's like you're putting a band-aid on the thing."

"Sweets, why would I buy a new TV when we have a perfectly good one that just needs a little love and care?" James asks, still into the show. "I'll look at it after the show goes off."

Tracy is amazed as she watches her husband continuing to focus on the TV.

"You know who else could use some love and care?" Tracy asks with a smirk on her face. "Your wife. I swear sometimes I think you're married to that TV instead of me."

"What was that, Sweets?" James asks, barely paying attention to his wife.

"I said I think you're married to that TV instead of me," she repeats, causing a quick nod from her husband.

"That's nice," James replies. "Hey, can you do me a favor and keep it down? I'm trying to watch the show."

It's clear to Tracy that she's wasting her time as she gets up and makes her way back into the dining room area. She sighs as she looks at her work and hears the TV in the background. She's emotionally drained as she takes a seat to try and work through the distractions going on in her home. As James watches the show, an advertisement comes on the screen saying that the show is looking for new contestants for the next season. His eyes light up with excitement as he quickly locates his cell phone and pulls up the web address on the screen. He fills out the application with a glimmer of hope in his eyes before hitting the submit button. He's about to put his phone down when an idea hits him. He looks at Tracy, who is struggling with her work, with a smirk on his face. He pulls the link back up on his phone and refreshes the link before inputting Tracy's information on the form as well.

Back in Dallas, Chris is sitting with his six-year-old son Anthony watching the Team Experiment show as well. They both are laughing watching one of the competitions going on within the show, when Chris's wife, Alexis, walks into the living room and notices them. While Alexis is everything Chris could hope for in a wife looks-wise, their personalities didn't mesh with each other as it once did. It was the reason Chris waited so long to get married. He wanted to be certain that she was the one for him, even though they had Anthony years prior. Their relationship seems to have gone stale, but outside of the one night fling with Tracy, he has been faithful to her. She shakes her head when she notices her husband and son wasting time.

"Chris, really?" She says as she crosses her arms. "You know Anthony shouldn't be watching all that TV."

"Cut him some slack, Lex," Chris responds, defending his son. "It's just a little fun on network television. It's nothing bad."

As timing would have it, one of the show's contestants goes into as explicit filled tirade, causing Alexis to frown at her husband. Chris nervously chuckles while scratching his head.

"I mean, they bleeped out all of the bad words, so it's not too bad," he tries to explain.

Alexis sighs before turning her attention towards Anthony.

"Anthony, go run your bath water and find your pajamas," she instructs. "I'll be up in a second."

Anthony gets up and quickly runs towards the bathroom to carry out his mother's instructions. Alexis turns her attention back toward her husband, looking at him as if she's disappointed.

"Chris, you know I don't like it when you do that. We need a united front when dealing with him. If he sees us at odds like that, it might give him the wrong impression," she says before taking a seat next to her husband.

"I get all that, but sometimes you gotta let a kid be a kid," Chris responds. "You got the boy spoiled with all this coddling. Watching a little TV isn't gonna kill the boy."

Alexis sighs as she lays her head on her husband's shoulder and turns her attention towards the TV.

"You and this reality TV," she says, trying to understand her husband's fascination with the genre. "Which one is this one?"

"It's called Team Experiment. All these random people live in one house competing with each other for one million dollars," Chris explains. "A bunch of crazy competitions and trivia and stuff. It's crazy."

"Let me guess, they have at least one loud ass black contestant," Alexis quips.

"That would be Sasha," Chris points out as Sasha appears on the screen, cussing out several people. "Fine as hell, but has a mouth on her, for real."

Alexis chuckles as she cuddles in with her husband.

"So, I was thinking, after we put Anthony to bed, me and you can have some alone time," she says, smirking. "I wouldn't mind Lil' Chris making a visit tonight."

Chris' eyes light up with his wife's proposal.

"I think Lil' Chris would be cool making a delivery tonight," he replies. "I think we can dig out some of the toys to help us out too. I'm feeling a little kinky."

Alexis's mood changes, as it so often does when Chris suggest using their sex toys.

"I was just thinking about something nice and normal," she admits. "I mean, I gotta work tomorrow, and so do you. We don't have time for all of that."

"We never have time for it," Chris quips as his mood changes as well. "I mean seriously, when is a good time? I suggest it on the weekends, and you're either tired or on your period. I suggested it on our last vacation away, and you thought the hotel walls were too thin and didn't want to make a scene. Apparently, you didn't mind the paper-thin walls when you were hollering at the top of your lungs when we did have sex. I'm just saying, Lex, when is the right time for us to have a little fun? Please, tell me."

Alexis chuckles before kissing her husband on the nose.

"We'll figure something out later. Okay?" She says, brushing her husband's thoughts to the side. "Right now, after Anthony is done taking his bath, I'll get him ready for bed. Once he's done, I expect you and Lil' Chris to be in the room ready."

Chris is about to respond, but Alexis quickly jumps up and heads towards the bathroom to make sure Anthony is running his water as she instructed him. A disappointed Chris turns his attention back towards the TV just as the show advertises they are looking for new contestants. He thinks for a moment before pulling out his cell phone and loading the website. He quickly adds his information to the questionnaire hoping for selection to add some excitement to an otherwise boring life.

The sun is shining brightly on the California coast with a perfect seventy-five-degree day currently underway. At WBC Studios in Burbank, several TV executives are all having their weekly meeting going over ratings, successes, and failures for the station. In the group is Team Experiment Producer, Jonathan Dunbar, and Studio Head, Monty Brooks, who are all listening to one of the successful executives discussing his show. Dunbar has a hint of sweat filling his brow as he awaits his turn. He is the head executive for the Team Experiment show. He's currently struggling as the numbers for the show has been down for the fourth consecutive month. He knows, based on the ever-changing platform of network television, that not only was the show in danger of getting canceled, but he was also in the hot seat after multiple failed shows under his watch. The group claps as the other executive wraps up his presentation before Brooks looks towards Dunbar.

"Alright, Jon. The floor is yours," he says to a nervous Dunbar, who rises from his chair.

The pudgy executive tries to calm himself before going into his presentation.

"Thank you, Mr. Brooks. Well, it's no secret that the Team Experiment Brand has been struggling with its intended demographic. The production crew and I have some great ideas where we can not only increase our thirty-five to forty-five market hold, but even expand our reach to the younger, more lucrative eighteen to thirty-four group," Dunbar says, trying to downplay the negative results. "I think by this time next year, you're looking at a whole new revamped show with different competitions and twists the likes that haven't been seen on network television in decades. Team Experiment is going to come back, ladies and gents! New and improved, and full of plot lines that will have you glued to your seat!"

Dunbar nervously smiles as the rest of the room looks confused. One of the executives raises his hand.

"Yeah, Ted," Dunbar responds.

"Yeah, you mentioned this before this year's season that you had an ace up your sleeve trying to reach out to that younger audience. As I recall, you brought Sasha to the program to help with that demographic," Ted points out before Dunbar quickly waves him off.

"Sasha was a trial basis," he quickly answers. "I'll admit that was our fault. Well, not me, of course. It was our casting director's fault, so to speak. We thought she would bring in a certain element and were disappointed it didn't work in our favor."

"Yeah, per our data, she used the word *fuck* and its derivatives one hundred and forty-seven times," Ted points out, reading from a sheet he had with him.

"Oh. Well, over a season, that average isn't that bad," a nervous Dunbar replies. "But as you can see, we've-"

"I'm sorry to interrupt, but that was one hundred and forty-seven times in just last night's aired show," Ted corrects.

"Well, it's a good thing we have the sensor, boys," Dunbar responds with a nervous laugh. "I mean, we got to have something for them to do, am I right?"

Dunbar's attempt at levity falls flat to everyone in the meeting as Ted shakes his head.

"I don't see how that's funny in any way," he responds as a jittery Dunbar stands silently in front of the group. "What I was getting at is you said you have new ideas. Sasha was a new idea and obviously hasn't panned out. If anything, we've lost more viewers than we earned during that time slot. My question is, what new ideas do you have for the next season?"

"Well, we have a few preliminary ideas we're still sorting out, but as soon as we cut through all the red tape, I'll make sure you're the first to know," Dunbar responds, hoping that the line of questioning goes away quickly.

Brooks frowns as he's had enough of Dunbar's lack of accountability.

"Could you all give us the room, please?" He asks the other executives.

As they all empty the room, Dunbar and Ted briefly make eye contact as Dunbar shoots him an evil look. After the room is cleared, Brooks takes a moment to look over several documents before addressing his subordinate. Dunbar despised his boss because Brooks was everything that he wasn't. He was sickened by the fact that Brooks could afford to wear a different top of the line thousand dollar suit daily. Even though he was younger than Brooks, you wouldn't know it. Brooks was in shape with a hint of grayness flowing through his hair, making him look more distinguished. In contrast, Dunbar was short and pudgy, wearing the same off the rack suit with different shirts daily, and fully bald on the top of his head. All he's ever wanted to be was a player in Hollywood, but his time might be up. Brooks clears his throat before addressing Dunbar.

"Jon, I'm not going to sugarcoat this. Your numbers are terrible. When I let you take over this show, we were in the top ten at our time slot weekly. Now, we're lucky if we reach the top fifty," Brooks points out. "In this city, with the string of losses that you've had in the last six or so years, it's not out of line to think you may be a little out of touch with reality, no pun intended."

"Mr. Brooks, it's difficult with all these new avenues of entertainment," Dunbar explains. "Folks today spend more time watching YouTube than they do network television."

"Be that as it may, there were certain expectations you were to achieve, and you've fallen flat on all of them," Brooks responds, sending fear into the heart of Dunbar. "Currently, you're under contract for one final season. You have one final chance to make this show a hit. If not, well, I hope you have other fulfilling talents because nobody in this city will hire you again. Not with your history. Am I making myself clear?"

Dunbar nods his head as Brooks smiles and rises from his seat.

"Wonderful. I can't wait to see some of those new ideas you were talking about today," he says before making his way out of the conference room.

Dunbar sighs as he begins to panic, not knowing his next move. After a few moments of stress, he quickly grabs his phone and calls his assistant.

"Margie, it's me," he says as she answers the phone. "I want you to bring all the profiles of the new contestants to my office. We have a long night ahead of us. We're going to break down each and every one of them until we have a perfect cast."

"Tonight? Mr. Dunbar, I already have plans tonight," Margie responds. "I have a date."

"Cancel it," Dunbar snaps back. "If we don't get this next season right, we're both are going to be canceled, if you know what I mean."

After a few moments of silence, Margie finally responds.

"Okay, fine," she replies, unenthused. "I'll take care of it."

Dunbar hangs up the line and hurries off to his office, awaiting the arrival of his assistant.

Hours later, Dunbar and Margie, who has arrived with all the paperwork of prospects, are sitting together at Dunbar's desk sifting through the applications trying to find the next crop of contestants. Dunbar is frustrated as he looks at Margie and her Velma from Scooby-Doo like appearance equipped with her oversized glasses frames and short auburn bob hair. She dresses a little more provocative than her cartoon doppelganger, but still had a nerdy personality to her, which annoyed her boss.

"This is hopeless," he says, throwing down a file. "There must be a million profiles here. How are we supposed to manage this? All I see are more Sasha's in the bunch."

"Did you see the teaser for the next episode?" Margie asks while adjusting her glasses. "Apparently, she lunged at one of the other contestants with a knife overnight. They've been teasing it all day."

"Well, that'll help with tonight's episode at least," Dunbar points out. "No, what we need is some sort of niche gimmick that draws people in. Something that will appeal to the masses, but draw our base in. It has to be a gimmick, not the people that have to draw viewers in."

Dunbar takes a looks at his demographics once more and sifts through the break downs when something catches his eyes.

"Seems like our biggest draw is with the married households," he deduces. "We use a lot of singles on our past shows, haven't we?"

"Yes, because you said that married people aren't a draw, and we'd be wasting our time using married folks," Margie points out. "You said something along the lines that 'married people aren't attractive enough to be on television' if I recall."

Dunbar frowns as he continues to look through the ratings paperwork.

"Well, clearly they watch the show," he points out. "Let's make this easy. Let's sort these out by eliminating the single contestants."

"You want the show with married couples?" A confused Margie asks.

"No, not couples, just no singles. We can work the family angle, showing their spouses and children throughout the broadcast, and even interviews! I can see it now. We can build competitions around them spending time with their spouses or something and build storylines off of that. It's genius!"

"I thought we were looking to pull in the eighteen to thirty-four demo?" Margie reminds her boss.

"That's what I told them in the meeting today, but it's impossible to figure out what Millennials and Generation Z viewers like. It's all about YouTube this, and Call of Duty that with them," Dunbar replies. "If married couples like watching our show, I say we cater to them and try to bring more of that. There's still a lot of advertisement money to be made with the married demographic. Besides, we tried Sasha to cater to the eighteen to thirty-four demOgraphic. See how good that worked out?"

Margie rolls her eyes, unmoved by Dunbar's excuses, before she goes onto her computer and filters out the non-married applicants.

"Alright, that eliminates a little more than half of the applicants," she says, adjusting her glasses once more. "That's good, but we still need something else to filter down by."

Dunbar thinks for a moment before snapping his fingers.

"What state were you born in?" He asks.

"Texas? Why?"

"Let's go with a Texas only cast. See how many we have after that," Dunbar says.

Margie nods her head and types the information into the computer and is amazed by the results.

"That eliminated over two-thirds of our applicants. I think you're on to something here," she says with a smirk.

"Great. Never knew you were a Texas girl. Seemed more like someone from New Hampshire or somewhere like that," Dunbar quips, causing Margie to frown.

"What's that supposed to mean?" She inquires.

"Oh, nothing! I'm not trying to sexually harass you or anything like that," Dunbar responds, backing down. "I don't need any of the 'me too' stuff happening around me. Send the remaining applicants the standard follow up application and survey. I want some interesting good looking contestants, but nothing Sasha like. Let me know when you get responses. Anyway, I have plans for the night. Get these files cleaned up and out of here."

Margie is stunned as she watches her boss grab his jacket and walk out of the office. She looks around at the files all over the office and frowns before shaking her head with disappointment.

Chapter 3

The Selection Process

It's a normal hot summer day in Dallas as Chris and Alexis are sitting at a local park protected by the shade of a nearby tree watching their son play with the other kids in the area at the jungle gym. Several other parents also surround the area trying to keep cool from the blazing sun while watching their kids run wild with each other. Alexis is wearing some extremely high jean shorts, which Chris looks at from the corner of his eye with a smirk on his face. He leers at her exposed legs and pedicured toes in her sandals, exciting him. Alexis glances over, notices her husband's look, and lifts her sunglasses to make eye contact with her husband.

"Really?" She said with a hint of attitude. "You looking at me like I'm a snack or something."

"Well, I could use a little bite to eat," Chris replies with a smirk. "I'm just saying, you out here in them daisy dukes looking like you want some attention. I'm happy to give it to you, for real."

"I am not out here looking for no damn attention," Alexis fires back. "It's hot as hell out here, so I wanted to wear something comfortable. That's it."

Chris shakes his head with a chuckle before looking around the playground area.

"Look around. Do you see any other woman dressed as provocative as you?" he says, turning his wife's attention to the surrounding area.

Alexis looks around and notices the more reserved dressing of the women in the area, with most wearing knee-high shorts or capris. There is one woman in a distance who is sitting alone on a bench wearing a skin-tight yellow sundress with heels on. Alexis smiles as she turns back to her husband.

"What about her?" She responds, pointing out the scantily dressed woman.

Chris looks at the female and chuckles.

"She doesn't count," he replies, smirking. "She's too young. She doesn't look like she even has kids."

"Oh, so you're trying to same I'm old now?" Alexis fires back.

"Here you go," Chris replies, shaking his head. "Always trying to start something. You know good and damn well that's not what I meant. All I'm saying is from the looks of it, she's a lot younger than a lot of these women here. I swear you old women love twisting folks words, don't you?"

Alexis starts laughing as Chris manages a chuckle himself. Alexis glances over at the scantily dressed female once again as the smile from her face slowly fades.

"I remember when my body was that young," she says. "What I wouldn't give to go back to that."

"Lex, come on now. There isn't anything wrong with how you look," Chris responds. "I mean before ol' girl made her way over to that bench, guess who was the one all the guys was checking out? The redbone with the daisy dukes on."

Alexis giggles as she looks around and catches a glimpse of a few men checking her out just as her husband said.

"You don't seem to be bothered by all the eyes on me," she playfully responds.

"Nope. Cause I know I'm going home tonight and crush that body," Chris responds with confidence. "So let them look. It doesn't bother me not one bit."

Alexis giggles once more as she gets comfortable on the bench laying her head on her husband's shoulder, watching their son play on the monkey bars. With his wife relaxed, Chris decides to see how much she's willing to go for.

"So, about me crushing that body tonight... I have a few ideas in case you're interested," he says with a sly grin on his face. "Maybe we can try this new thing with the-"

"You see, that's why I don't want to get you started," Alexis says, cutting off her husband. "You can't just keep things simple, can you? It's always cuffs, or oils, or feathers, or a swing. I told you before you bought that damn swing that I wasn't going to do all that. Why do you have to make things so difficult? Why can't we have sex like normal people?"

Chris shakes his head with disbelief while chuckling.

"I can't with you," he replies. "I mean, there are other positions than missionary. It's like you're stuck in the eighteen hundreds with sex. Even the Puritans had better sex than me. Believe it or not, you're the one who isn't normal. Couples do all kinds of freaky shit now. Hell, how about we do something *really* off the wall, and have you get on top for once?"

Alexis is stunned by her husband's aggression as she looks around to make sure nobody is eavesdropping into their conversation. She can't believe his thoughts on the subject and the venue in which he chose to have the discussion.

"This is neither the time nor place to have this conversation," she quips.

"It never is with you," Chris replies as he gets up and walks off back towards the car, upsetting Alexis.

He leans on the outside of his car frustrated mentally, and sexually with his wife. While he is a little kinky, he doesn't consider himself as farfetched as she would have him believe. He has a healthy sexual appetite but doesn't feel Alexis tries to meet him halfway. He likes things interesting and new. Nothing frustrates him more than a boring sex life, and although he loves his wife, it was starting to disrupt their relationship. After a few moments, he pulls out his cell phone and starts checking his email. He's surprised when he notices an email from the Team Experiment show. His eyes light up as he learns that he's under consideration to join the new season. He quickly pulls up the survey form and begins filling it out.

Back in Houston, Tracy is lying on her couch after a hard day's work trying to unwind. She's so exhausted that she was only able to get one of her heels off before collapsing on the couch. With her pants unbuttoned and her hair slumped over the armrest of the couch, she's about to doze off until she hears her husband shouting with excitement from the other room. She jumps up wondering what all the fuss is about, almost twisting her ankle. She finally removes her other heel before making her way into the room where her husband is sitting behind their computer desk, filling out the Team Experiment survey form he received with glee.

"What the hell is going on?" Tracy asks as she tenderly walks over to her husband. "Why are you shouting like you won the lottery or something?"

"Shit, I might have!" James exclaims as he continues to fill out the survey. "I heard back from the Team Experiment folks! I'm under consideration to join the next season! Well, we both are."

"What do you mean, *we*?" A curious Tracy asks as she looks over her husband's shoulder.

"I filled out an application for you too," James answers. "I figure we'd double down on our chances if I put us both in the pot."

"Double down?" Tracy replies as if she's offended. "Why in the hell would you sign me up for something like that? It's full of nonsense!"

"Sweets, we're talking a million-dollar prize! Do you understand how life-changing that can be?" James asks. "Well, technically half a million since you have to split it with your partner, but I mean, we have a better chance of winning that than the lottery at this point! There was no way in hell I wasn't gonna put you in there."

Tracy rolls her eyes before looking at what her husband is typing into the survey.

"What the hell?" She says, looking confused. "What is all this stuff about you being a former gangbanger? James, I know you not just sitting here lying to these people?"

"You damn right I am," James says with a smirk on his face. "These shows don't want a mechanic who works in a garage. Nah, they want controversy. They want ignorance. Have you not seen Sasha on the show?"

Tracy rolls her eyes once more as she watches her husband completing his survey.

"Look, there's just a way things are done," James continues. "If you wanna get invited to the dance, you have to sweet talk your way in. When I get picked and win that half million, don't come crying to me about where's your cut if you're not gonna support your man."

Tracy sighs before hugging her husband from behind and kissing him on the cheek.

"Well, I wish you all the fortune you're seeking," she says.

James turns and looks at his wife with a smirk on his face as the two share a quick kiss.

"Say, I can go ahead and fill yours out if you want," he offers.

"No, that's quite alright. God knows what lies you'll tell them about me," Tracy responds.

"It wasn't gonna be that bad. Three kids, replaced hip, something along those lines," James says as he gets up from the desk. "I'm hungry. Did you start making dinner yet?"

Tracy looks at her husband and motions to him, bringing attention to the fact that she's still in her work clothes. James catches on and nods his head.

"Oh, my bad. Whenever you finished then," he says to his worn out wife. "Can you do lasagna? That sounds nice right about now."

Tracy sighs as James quickly heads to the living room, oblivious to his wife's mood. She takes a seat behind the computer and looks at the survey with her name on it. She reads the info where the show said contestants could spend up to forty-five days at their California location, which sways her interest slightly.

"Forty-five days away from the Texas heat and his ass? Shit, it might just be worth it," she says to herself with a smirk. "Alright, Team Experiment. Let's see if I can get lucky. Or at least let him get lucky so I can have a break."

Tracy giggles as she starts filling out the form fantasizing about palm trees, perfect weather, and alone time away from her neglectful husband.

In the WBC Studio conference room back in California, Dunbar and Margie are sitting next to each other busy sifting through the applicant surveys trying to come up with the perfect group of contestants to catch the viewers' eyes from their laptops. Dunbar chuckles as one survey catches his attention.

"Check this out. Look up James Styles," he says as Margie pulls up the survey on her laptop. "I can't believe someone would put on their survey about being an ex-gangbanger. I mean, where do they come up with this crap?"

"It's what they think we're looking for," Margie points out as she reads the profile as well. "I mean, he might have embellished just to catch our attention which worked since we're here talking about it. Or it may be true. You never can tell with these surveys."

"If it is true, he would have been perfect for my 'Gangsters in the Hood' proposal I pitched last year," Dunbar replies with Margie looking on confused. "You remember, the one about where we take ex-gangbangers to rival territories to see if they would make it? I'm telling you, it would have been a hit had they greenlit it."

"Let me guess, Fox?" Margie asks with a grin.

"Naturally," Dunbar answers with a chuckle before moving on to the next candidate.

Margie moves on as well when something catches her eyes.

"Hey, check out Tracy Styles. Seems like this is coming from the same household where the ex-gangbanger lives," she says as Dunbar pulls up the profile on his computer as well. "She looks like a winner. Simple, but cute. Normal profile, nothing too outlandish. She's a working-class woman and is part of the same demographic we're looking for. She looks good to me, what do you think?"

Dunbar reads over her questionnaire thoroughly before slowly nodding his head with agreement.

"I'm sure she has some skeletons in the closet being married to that nut job," Dunbar replies. "Maybe we can use that. 'Wife of a gangbanger' or 'Thug life, from a woman's perspective.' It could play. Add her to the show."

Margie rolls her eyes before taking down Tracy's name and moving on to her next applicant. After several moments Chris' profile catches her eye.

"Well, what do we have here?" She says with a smirk leering at Chris's photo. "I think I might have found our first guy. Chris Sargent, from Dallas. He's definitely eye candy for the ladies. Has a wife and child, decent profile, and did I mention he was eye candy for the ladies?"

Dunbar reads over Chris' profile before looking over towards Margie, who has an almost obsessive look as she looks at Chris's photo.

"Well, I guess he's won you over," Dunbar responds. "Cut scenes with him and his family would work. I guess if he's attractive enough for you, the rest of the scallywags will find him charming. Add him to the list."

Dunbar's words fall of deaf ears as Margie continues to leer at Chris' photo. Dunbar notices and grabs his head out of frustration before responding.

"Margie!" He exclaims, snapping his assistance from her thoughts.

"Sorry, sir," an embarrassed Margie responds. "I'll get on top of him—I mean on top of it. It, sir."

Margie chuckles nervously as Dunbar sighs.

"Alright, that's two down. Let's keep in moving," he says as Margie writes down Chris' name next to Tracy's.

The two network employees continue to sift through the names of the applicants trying to find other contestants as Tracy and Chris's name is written side by side, closer than the couple has been for over two years.

A little over a week later, Alexis is in the kitchen cooking dinner and watching Anthony from a distance when she hears Chris' cell phone ring. She walks over to the counter where he left the phone before jumping in the shower and checks the caller ID. The number isn't recognized. She curiously answers the phone before the call goes to voicemail.

"Hello?"

"Hello, I'm looking for Chris Sargent," Margie says on the other line.

"He's not available right now. I'm his wife. Can I help you?"

"Yes, this is Margie Weatherspoon with the WBC show Team Experiment. We received your husband's profile, and we'd like to extend him an invitation to be a contestant on our show," Margie says to a stunned Alexis.

"Team Experiment? You mean the show Team Experiment? The one on TV?" An excited Alexis responds.

"The very same, ma'am. Is there any way I can leave my contact information with you?" Margie asks as a frantic Alexis looks around the kitchen area for a pen and paper.

"I'm ready. Go ahead," she says.

She quickly jots down the information struggling to contain her excitement.

"I got it. I'll let him know to call you as soon as I can," Alexis says before hanging up the line and yelling in excitement.

She quickly runs to the bathroom and barges in, interrupting Chris' shower. He looks at her, confused as she struggles to get her words together.

"Are you okay?" He calmly asks.

"Oh my god, Chris, they called! They really called!" An excited Alexis exclaims causing more confusion between the couple.

"Define *they*," Chris asks as Alexis tries to gather herself.

"The show! The... the Team Experiment show! I just got off the line with one of their people! They want you to be on the show! They want you to be on the next season!" She blurts out, stunning her husband.

"Are... are you serious?" He asks with a smile. "You're not trying to punk me, are you?"

Alexis jumps into the shower with her husband and kisses him passionately, catching him off guard, getting soaked in the process.

"Shit, this isn't a joke," Chris says with a chuckle. "Holy shit, they want me on the show!"

"Yes! Oh my god, could you imagine what we could do with that money if we won?" Alexis replies as Chris looks at her strangely.

"If *we* won?" He asks with a smirk. "What do you mean, *we*? You said it was trash TV or something along those lines. Said it was bullshit."

"Baby, if I can get a half million dollars off that show, then it can be whatever the hell it wants to be," Alexis responds before rubbing on her husband's suds-soaked body. "Damn, seeing you like this makes me wanna, I don't know."

"Well, it's all here waiting for you," Chris flirts as Alexis begins running her fingers down towards his mid-section.

"It sure is," she replies, grasping his manhood.

Alexis starts getting undressed before Chris smells something in the air.

"What's that burning?" He asks, causing Alexis to panic.

"Oh shit! The chops!" She yells before jumping out of the shower and running back towards the kitchen.

Chris chuckles as he goes back to his shower excited to know that he's going to be on a show he knows and loves.

Later that night in Houston, Tracy sighs as she enters her dark apartment worn out from another hard day at work. As she cuts on the light, she's startled when she notices James sitting in the dark on the living room couch.

"James! You scared the shit out of me!" She exclaims as she calms down. "Why are you in here sitting in the dark?"

"The Team Experiment people called today," a somber James answers.

"Well, that's great, isn't it? I mean, you've always wanted

to be on the show, right?" Tracy asks with a smile until she notices her husband's mood. "Wait, are you looking like that because they rejected you?"

"Yeah, they rejected me, but they didn't reject you," James replies, shocking his wife. "They want you to be on the show. Can you believe that shit? You don't even watch the show, and they picked you to be a contestant. I swear life just doesn't work out for me."

Tracy can tell her husband is upset with the rejection. She tosses her things on the coffee table and sits next to him, snuggling in closely, trying to show a little affection.

"I'm sorry, hon. I know you really wanted this," she said, trying to empathize with him. "It's not that serious. I'll pass on the show. Only reason I filled that thing out was because you wanted me to. If you're not going, then the hell with it."

James looks at his wife as if he's offended by her words.

"Are you crazy?" He asks. "Of course you're going on the show! Why wouldn't you?"

"Because I don't want to," Tracy responds. "I don't want to be on some reality show. I don't want my life broadcast to the world. I honestly didn't think they'd pick me. I'm too boring for them, and I made sure to look that way on the survey. This is your thing, not mine."

Tracy gets up from the couch and makes her way to the bedroom followed closely by James.

"Sweets, it's a half-million," he points out. "Do you know what we can do with a half-million dollars?"

"Pay taxes on it mostly," Tracy responds as she starts to undress from her work clothes. "I mean, think about it, you're going to get taxed twice on it. Once when we receive the money, and another time when we file our taxes next year. You forget

I'm an accountant now. I see this type of thing all the time. We'd be lucky to net a couple hundred thousand after it's all said and done."

"Okay, I'd take the two hundred," James replies, amazed his wife doesn't see the benefits. "You can't tell me we can't use the money."

"We can always use more money," Tracy responds as she puts on her nightclothes. "I'm just not willing to sell my soul to get it. And you're assuming I'm gonna win? What if I don't? It would be a waste of time."

"Sweets, let me break this down to you," James says as he gently grabs his wife's arm to get her full attention. "You have a one and ten chance of winning this money. One and ten chance of winning a half-million dollars, or two hundred thousand as you call it. When are you ever gonna get better odds than that?"

"James, it's not about the money. It's never about that," Tracy explains. "One out of ten aside, I don't want to be on TV. It just scares me."

"Come on, sweets. Do it for me. Please," James replies as he starts to fondle his wife's body. "Please. Just this one time, do it for me."

Tracy begins to falter as her husband's touch weakens her. James knew how to work her over to get what he wants, and with affection between her and husband being far and few in-between, a simple touch weakened her. As James starts kissing her on her neck, Tracy nods her head with agreement.

"Okay, I'll do it," she says, giving in to his touch. "I'll do the show."

James smiles as he begins undressing his wife. He leads her over to the bed and drops his pants before quickly inserting himself inside her. The passion has Tracy excited as her husband begins to pleasure her. The moment is short-lived, however, as James quickly orgasms, much to his wife's surprise. After a few more pumps, James collapses on top of his disappointed wife with a smirk on his face. He gives her a quick kiss on the nose as Tracy lies in bed, emotionless after the quick sexual encounter.

Chapter 4

Reunion

The Team Experiment house is set up and ready for filming with the production set to begin that day. The house is almost mansion-like with multiple rooms and living areas built for comfort. The back yard is massive as well equipped with a pool and a workout area taking advantage of the beautiful California weather. Several film crew members are making their way around the room making last-minute adjustments as Tracy is sitting alone in the lobby looking around.

"I must be out of my mind doing this," she says to herself as she watches the crew members around her.

Margie is directing a few of the crew members when she notices Tracy sitting in the lobby looking confused. She quickly makes her way over and greets her.

"Tracy, right?" Margie asks as Tracy rises and shakes the assistant's hand.

"Hey, yes," she replies.

"Hello, I'm Margie, one of the show assistants. Sorry it took me so long to greet you, but last-minute changes always seem to come up," Margie explains as she looks at one of the film crew setting up close by. "Did someone give you the grand tour of the house?"

"Oh, yeah. It's a lovely house," Tracy says as the two begin walking towards the living room area.

"So, do you know how the show works?" Margie inquires.

"Not really. My husband is the Team Experiment fan. I've only seen bits and pieces of it when he's watching," Tracy admits.

"Yeah, it's something we're trying to fix," Margie responds. "We're trying to broaden our demographics and make this a show more wholesome, so to speak. That's why this season we're only dealing with married couples. In the past, we've had a few rough contestants, so to speak."

"Yeah, I saw Sasha," Tracy responds, causing Margie to giggle.

"Everyone knows her, don't they?" Margie says as she offers Tracy a seat at the island area in the kitchen. "Let me explain how this works. We start off with ten contestants, including you. Five men, five women. One of the five men will partner up with you as you compete with four other teams in various trivia or physical events throughout the week with the ability to earn points. At the end of every week, the team with the most points earns the right to nominate two teams to go into a sudden death competition. Whichever team losses that the sudden death round is sent home, while the other team lives to fight another week. Points reset each week to make sure there is a fair advantage, and there are several twists throughout the storyline."

Tracy nods her head with understanding as Margie continues.

"Now the show is live, and the entire house is wired for

both sound and video, with the exception of the Strategy Room. That room is where you and your partner can meet throughout the week and discuss strategy without anyone being able to overhear your plans. Some teams build alliances, some teams strategize based on where they are in the standings. It's a chess match, and usually, the smart teams make it to the end. Now, of course, the show has the right to make any rule changes it sees fit, and normally that leads to a twist or two."

"You mentioned twists once before. What do you mean by twists?" Tracy asks.

"Each year the show throws a couple of twists to spice up the story," Margie answers. "We normally don't decide that until the show is underway. Keeps the contestants on their toes. The show lasts forty-five days if you're the final team, and throughout that time, there is no contact with the outside world. There may be competitions that allow you to win a conversation with your family, but other than that, no outside world contact."

Tracy nods her head with understanding once again.

"That sucks," she says with a smirk.

"We reserve the right to use any footage in the home, so please try to not cuss or show any nudity while out in the main areas," Margie warns as Tracy looks at her confused.

"Um, so all that stuff with Sasha? Did she have the same speech, cause I'm thinking she didn't pay that much attention to the rules?" Tracy asks with a smirk.

"Sasha did get the same info you are, but Sasha is a special case," Margie replies with a grin. "Please don't tell me you're another Sasha."

"God no," Tracy replies with a chuckle. "I think I can go the distance without dropping f-bombs. I'm good."

"Great! So, did you have any questions?" Margie asks.

"When does the show begin?" Tracy asks.

"Well, you were the last contestant I had to meet with, so in about ten minutes," Margie responds, which shakes Tracy's nerves. "Hey, relax. It'll be fine. Just be you. A lot of people try to do too much when they're on these shows. We chose you because of your profile. We just want you to be you."

Tracy sighs before nodding her head.

"Oh, and by the way, unlike some of those other shows, our kitchen and pantry are fully stocked. So eat your heart out," Margie says with a smile. "So, I have your release forms and questionnaire all filled out, so you're good to go."

"Yeah, some of those questions were a little personal, don't you think?" Tracy asks.

"They can be, but you'll never know what we use them for, if we even use them at all," Margie explains. "I hope you were honest answering them."

"Yeah, I was. I mean, I just found it a little odd, that's all," Tracy responds.

"That's great. Well, you can hang out here until game time. We're going to reveal everyone together, so I don't want y'all getting friendly just yet. Stick around here. I'll send someone to get you when we're ready. Good luck," Margie says before shaking hands with Tracy and walking off.

A nervous Tracy sighs as she looks around the area wondering exactly what she's gotten herself into.

The viewing public are all in front of their TV sets waiting for the premiere episode of Team Experiment, including both Alexis and James. The show's intro starts with the show's host,

Melissa, who is dressed to perfection with her business suit, long curly hair, and makeup that blended flawlessly with her almond-colored skin, standing by with a smile.

"Hello, folks, and welcome to Team Experiment!" she says with enthusiasm standing in the back yard of the house. "I'm your host, Melissa, and you are in for a show today! This edition of Team Experiment is represented by the great state of Texas! As always, teams will battle each other for the chance to win one million dollars! We have five cowboys and five cowgirls looking to make their claim. As always, this season is filled with twists and turns, so make sure you tune in each week to see how our contestants handle those curveballs."

Melissa makes her way further into the back yard, where all the contestants are standing blindfolded. The men are standing on one side, and the women are standing on the other across from them. Melissa walks in the middle as she continues.

"Normally, we'd like our contestants to mingle a bit, and choose their partners, but in the first twist of the season, we've decided to let fate play a hand. Contestants, your partner is standing right across from you. You may now remove your blindfold to meet your partner," Melissa says.

Everyone removes their blindfold and looks over towards their partner. Mitch is standing across from Tracy. He walks over and introduces himself as the two shake hands. Tracy is impressed with Mitch, who was solidly built and a white guy. She felt that will work better in her odds in the physical competition. The smile on her face is short-lived when she turns to her right and notices Chris shaking hands with the other contestants. She looks as if she's seen a ghost. Chris looks up and notices her as well, which stuns him. The two share a look before some of the production workers wave them over to stand in their next positions. Dunbar, who is watching the show from inside the house, notices the glare between the two and grabs his chin, pondering what he just saw.

"Interesting," he says to himself as he continues to watch Tracy's reaction.

Melissa walks over to Tracy and Mitch with a smile as she looks towards the cameras.

"Okay, now that our teams have met, let's introduce them to you folks at home," she says before turning her attention to Mitch. "This is team number one! Give us your name, where you're from, and what you do for a living."

'My name is Mitch, and I'm from Tyler, Texas. I'm currently working as a forklift operator, and I'm ready to rock and roll!" An excited Mitch says before Melissa turns her attention to Tracy.

"Okay, Mitch, that's the enthusiasm we like to hear. And who's your partner over here?" She says to a still stunned Tracy.

"Hi. I'm, um, Tracy. I'm from Dallas, well I was born in Dallas, but I live in Houston now, and I'm... I'm an accountant for... for a major firm," Tracy stutters as she struggles to get over seeing Chris.

Melissa chuckles as she notices Tracy's nervousness.

"Relax, Tracy. You look as if you've seen a ghost," she says, trying to calm Tracy down.

"I'm... I'm just a little nervous," Tracy says.

"Well, you better shake it off because the other teams aren't going to have any leniency with you. Good luck, team one!" Melissa says before making her way to the next team.

Inside the home, watching the introductions from the window, Margie is making sure everything is going on without a hitch. Dunbar makes his way over to her and pulls her to the side.

"Did you see the look on Tracy's face?" He asks Margie. "Something's not right."

"I'm sorry, sir, but I've been trying to focus on making sure the production goes smoothly," Margie reminds her boss. "Besides, I didn't see anything. She was the last one I met up with. I think she's just nervous, that's all."

"I'm telling you it wasn't nerves; it was something else," Dunbar responds as he continues to watch Tracy from the window.

"Be that as it may, what do you want me to do about it now?" Margie quips back. "You want me to pull her off live on air?"

Dunbar thinks for a moment as he continues to watch the show from a distance.

"No. Let's let it play out and see where it goes. In the meantime, cross-check all of the contestants on the show," Dunbar says. "Someone in this house has her running scared, and I want to know who."

"Done," Margie quickly responds, looking to end the conversation. "I think you're overreacting, but I'll take care of it. Now, can I please get back to my duties that I'm underpaid for?"

Dunbar nods his head as Margie walks off to talk to one of the production managers. A smirk enters Dunbar's face as he continues to obsess over Tracy, hoping that he's found his story-line for the season.

Back in the yard, Melissa has made her way down to the final team of Chris and Julia.

"And finally, introducing team five," she says as she looks towards Julia.

"Hey, my name is Julia, I'm from Amarillo, and I'm a cashier. I can taste that million dollars, so the rest of y'all better be ready cause I'm coming for you!"

Melissa nods her head enjoying Julia's enthusiasm before turning her attention towards Chris.

"My name is Chris, I'm from Dallas, and I'm a store manager," Chris answers as Melissa nods her head.

"Well, good luck, team five," Melissa responds before looking back towards the camera. "Which one of our teams will start out with a bang, and which one of our teams will start out with a thud? Find out as today's first competition begins after these messages."

The camera operator yells clear as Melissa's smile immediately drops before she heads over to get her makeup touched up. The contestants all begin to mingle with each other as Chris and Tracy keep their distance without looking too obvious at each other. Team two consists of the cute older and reserved homemaker, Monica, who is from Houston, and Gerald, a skinny blonde haired bus driver from Galveston. Team three is David, a young attractive waiter from Fort Worth, and the drop-dead gorgeous, Lucia from El Paso, who works as a freelance photographer. Victoria, the sexy and scantily dressed Instagram model from Arlington, and the short but solidly built Sebastian, a laborer from Austin, make up team four. As they continue to talk with each other, Mitch takes center stage as he addresses all the competitors.

"Hey, guys. Look, I know this is a competition and everything, but I want to wish everyone here good luck, and may the best team win," he says.

"Trust me, we intend to. Isn't that right, Lucy?" David says to his teammate.

"It's Lucia," she corrects. "And yes, we plan on whippin' that ass all up and down this joint, so y'all bet not get too friendly."

"Now that's what I like," David responds, speaking more of his Lucia's looks more than anything else.

"Spoken like true runner ups," Gerald fires back with a chuckle. "That money is ours."

"Yeah, I think we have a pretty good chance," Monica says, chiming in with her new teammate. "I've seen every Team Experiment episode since the beginning. I know every trick they will throw at us."

"Just what I like to see," Mitch says with a smirk. "Nice and healthy competition! Don't worry, I'll invite all of you to my house to celebrate after me and Tracy take this thing."

Everyone laughs as they continue to boast their superiority towards each other. David looks towards Chris and Julia and notices they're being quiet talking amongst themselves.

"Well, I see you two are being awfully quiet right now," he says, bringing the other's attention towards Chris and Julia. "What are y'all doing down there? Plotting already?"

"We're all business this way. Aren't we, Chris?" Julia says, looking towards her partner.

"Um, yeah. All business," Chris responds with a nervous chuckle. "Let's get it."

One of the production assistants walks over and gets the team members to stand together as the show is almost back from break. A newly fresh made up, Melissa rejoins the contestants and takes center stage between them as the camera crew counts down their return from commercial.

"Welcome back," Melissa says with a smile as she looks around at the contestants. "Now that we've met our cast for this season, what better way to kick things off than with our first competition! I hope y'all are ready to get wet!"

All the contestants clap their hands as Melissa leads them to the middle of the yard where their first competition is set up. There is a table with plastic cups and rope on top located about twenty feet away from the pool. On the ground is a small bucket, one for each team.

"Alright, for this competition we're going to have a simple fill the bucket with water exercise," Melissa explains to the cast. "Ladies, your job is to take the plastic cups, fill it with water, and pour the cup into the bucket as quickly as you can. The first person to fill their team's bucket wins. Seems simple right?"

The female contestants nod their heads with approval.

"Now, you know we can't make it that easy, right?" Melissa responds with a grin. "Through this exercise, your hands will be tied behind you back, meaning you can only use your mouth to carry the cups."

The women have several different reactions as Melissa turns her attention towards the guys.

"Men, we haven't forgotten about you," she says with a sinister smirk filling her face. "You're going to be the ladies Uber in a sense. Each of you will mount on all fours and deliver the ladies to the drop area and back. Your passenger can only dismount once you make it to the red lines by the pool and by the buckets. You must repeat the process until your team's bucket is filled."

All the men confidently nod their heads except for Gerald, who looks at Monica's full-figured frame and wonders how he's going be able to balance her with his skinny body.

"The winner of this contest gets one hundred points, and if it's done under five minutes, we'll double that to two hundred points!" Melissa says before turning her attention back towards the camera.

All the contestants clap, excited for their first even. Tracy and Chris finally make eye contact with each other as Melissa hears something in her earpiece and turns to the cast once again.

"You know what, folks? I'm feeling good today, and I'm going to throw one more twist in the mix for today's event," she says, grabbing everyone's attention. "I'm going to officially declare today men's day! The male of the team that wins today's event will get two hours to spend in the strategy room to interview each of the show's female contestants. At the end of the week, he'll get the option of trading partners if he finds a better fit than his current partner. However, I'd advise that winner to be careful because this same option may come up for the women later down the line. The first elimination battle is in two weeks, so let's get this battle underway!"

All the contestants mingle once more, shaking each other's hands wishing their competitors luck. Tracy and Chris finally are face to face with each other. They both have a million thoughts running through their minds before shaking each other's hands.

"Good luck," Chris says, trying to keep up their charade of not knowing each other.

"Yeah, you too," Tracy responds.

As she tries to move along, Chris doesn't let her go as he looks around.

"I need to win this," he whispers to her.

"Shhhh. Keep your voice down. The record everything here," she whispers back as Chris finally releases her hand.

Tracy hurries off to the starting line and joins her partner Mitch and has her hands tied behind her back in preparation for the competition.

"Hey, you coming?" Julia says, snapping Chris's from his gaze of Tracy.

"Huh, oh. Yeah. Let's do this," Chris responds as he makes his way over towards the starting line prepping for the event.

All teams are set at the starting line with the men on all fours waiting for the event to get underway. The women have their cups grasped firmly between their teeth, ready to go as well. The short commercial break has ended as Melissa rejoins the cast to get the event underway. Chris shares a look with Tracy once more hoping she's all in with letting him win. Chris figures that she and Mitch would be his biggest competition with the great shape Mitch was in. He takes a deep breath and begins to focus as Melissa smiles once more for the camera.

"And we're back," she says before turning her attention towards the cast. "Ladies and gentlemen, are we ready to go?"

All the contestants give a thumbs up or a head nod.

"Alright, here we go. On your mark. Get set. Go!" Melissa exclaims, starting the competition.

The race is off as Julia is the first to saddle Chris as the two move fast out of the gate, followed closely by Mitch and Tracy trying to reach the pool. The teams of David, Lucia, and Sebastian, Victoria battle it out for third place, as Gerald struggles to move Monica's plus size body down the course. After a few moments of struggling to balance Monica, Gerald's body gives out, causing Monica to fall to the side.

"Gerald and Monica, you have to start over," Melissa instructs. "Hurry!"

Gerald and Monica both rise from the ground and sprint back to the starting point to attempt once again. While they are resetting, Chris and Julia have made their first return as Julia dismounts Chris and does her best to balance the cup in her mouth before dumping its contents into her team's bucket. Chris is trying to catch his breath when Mitch and Tracy pull alongside him. Tracy is much faster with her dismount than Julia was as the two teams were off to the races once again towards the pool.

"Chris and Julia are moving at lightning speed as they're on their way back towards the pool," Melissa says, calling the play by play. "Nipping at their heels is the team of Tracy and Mitch, followed by teams three and four who keep battling back and forth for third place. Taking up the rear is team two who just can't seem to get things going so far."

Gerald collapses once again as he's out of breath. Monica frowns, realizing that they are essentially eliminated from the competition. Several back and forth trips later, Chris is starting to show signs of fatigue as he makes his latest drop off towards the pool, followed closely by Mitch and Tracy. Julia quickly dumps her head in the water getting her cup filled as much as possible before making her way back to Chris who is gasping for air. They take off, but not as quickly as they would like. Tracy quickly fills her cup and jumps on Mitch's back. Her and Mitch quickly take off back towards their bucket, making up ground with Chris and Julia.

"Unbelievable! Team's one and five are neck and neck thanks to the quick pool transition by Tracy," Melissa says as she watches both teams head to the finish line. "It seems Chris is slowing down. He may not have enough to finish strong."

Chris is gasping trying to keep pace and make it to the red line. Both teams only need a little water to fill their bucket so it's coming down to this final lap. Mitch is still moving strongly as he finally has enough drive to move ahead of Chris. Tracy glances at Chris and can tell he's fading fast. Mitch is almost at the finish line when Tracy purposely falls off his back to allow Chris and Julia to take the lead.

"Oh no, Tracy fell off several feet away from the finishing line," an excited Melissa says. "That leaves the window open for Chris and Julia to finish this thing!"

Julia is cheering on Chris as he fights through exhaustion, making it right over the red line, allowing Julia to jump off and dump her water into the bucket filling it to its capacity, winning the show's first competition. Julia starts jumping around in celebration as a gassed Chris turns on his back and pumps his fist in excitement.

"It's over! Team five takes the first competition!" Melissa exclaims as she makes her way over by Julia and Chris, who's finally managed to sit up.

"Let's get a word from our winners here. Chris, I know you're tired. It looked like you were going to win this thing easily, but at the end, Mitch gave you a run for your money," she says, crouching down as best she can to keep Chris in the camera frame.

"We got off to a great start, but you gotta give team one credit," Chris says, still trying to catch his breath. "They made a hell of a comeback at the end there. Hats off to them."

"Well, you didn't get the double point bonus, but you did win the option to swap teammates if you so choose," Melissa reminds him. "If you decide to change up, the points follow Julia to her new partner. You two worked well together today. Any chance you're looking to change up?"

Chris smiles as he looks at all the other contestants.

"Julia was a real trooper. We'll see what the future holds," he replies before Melissa stands and turns her attention to Julia.

"Now, Julia, you seem very excited. No matter what happens, you've solidified yourself one hundred points. What was your strategy going into this event?" She asks her.

"I just wanted to focus on keeping the cup in my mouth as tightly as I could," Julia responds with a giggle. "It's not as easy as it looks while trying to balance yourself on someone's back."

"Now that Chris has the power to change teammates, do you'll think he'll use it?" Melissa inquires.

"Not if he wants to win," Julia replies, playfully tapping Chris on his shoulder.

Melissa smiles as she takes a look at the camera once more.

"There you have it, folks. Team five takes the day with an awesome last-minute comeback. We'll be back after these messages.

Melissa and the camera crew make their way to a new location as Mitch walks over and helps Chris to his feet.

"Good game," he says as the two shake hands.

"Yeah, you too," Chris responds.

"I thought we had you. Tracy just lost her balance at the worst possible time. We'll get you next time though," Mitch responds as Chris looks over at Tracy, who is conversing with the other contestants.

"Yeah. It's funny how things work out," Chris replies with a chuckle.

Chris and Mitch rejoin the rest of the group who are gathering at the outside lounging area. Inside the home, Dunbar pulls Margie to the side once again, much to her confusion.

"Did you see that?! Tell me you saw that!" Dunbar exclaims.

"Saw what?" A confused Margie asks.

"Tracy! She fell off on purpose," Dunbar accuses. "It was

obvious! Didn't you see it?"

"Boss, I think you've had a long day," Margie calmly says, ignoring Dunbar's words. "All I saw was a lady possibly getting a little too excited and lost her balance at the end. It made for good TV in my opinion. I mean, why would she purposely lose? There's a lot of money on the line."

"I know what I saw, Margie," an insistent Dunbar fires back. "Have you looked into her yet like I asked?"

"You mean as in thirty minutes ago when you asked me to cross-check her with everyone in the house?" A sarcastic Margie responds. "Sure, I had plenty of time to take care of that while also running a show."

"Well, get on it! I smell something here, and it might be what we need to give this season legs if we play it right," Dunbar replies.

Margie rolls her eyes and walks off as Dunbar turns his attention back towards Tracy. He strokes his goatee trying to figure out exactly what's going on with her, and how he can use it to his benefit.

Chapter 5

Feelings of Old

Melissa is standing in the back yard with Chris as the camera gives them a countdown to returning live on national TV. The other contestants are still sitting in the lounging area after the hard-fought competition from earlier.

"Welcome back to Team Experiment. I'm standing here with one half of today's winner, Chris from team five," she says to the camera before turning her attention towards Chris. "Now, as promised, today you get to use your powers to interview any of the other team's ladies in the strategy room. You'll get to interview the other three ladies in the next few days, but for right now, who is up first?"

Chris looks over to the lounge area and acts as though he's trying to figure out who his next selection will be. He's thrown off a little as Victoria shoots him a seductive look but turns his attention back towards Melissa.

"Tough decision, but I'll start off with Tracy since she came real close to beating us today," Chris replies.

Melissa waves Tracy over, who is reluctant to join initially, but slowly makes her way over next to Chris.

"Okay, Tracy, Chris has chosen you to interview first in the strategy room. You have only a couple of hours together at the most, so it's important that you learn all you can about each other in order to see if this partnership would fit," Melissa says as Tracy nods her head with a forced smile upon her face.

Chris struggles to hold in his laughter at Melissa's comments as she motions them to head inside the house.

"For the rest of our contestants, the day is done. Enjoy the food and other amenities that we have to offer in the Team Experiment House," Melissa says to the rest of the cast before turning her attention back to the camera. "Will Chris decide to change team members? Find out on next week's episode of Team Experiment! Good night everyone!"

The smile from Melissa's face instantly drops once the show is off air as she looks at one of the lighting assistants.

"Are you kidding me?" She says to him with an attitude. "I mean were you trying to blind me with that reflection? Fix it, or I swear to god the next thing you'll be lighting is a flashlight in your own coffin!"

The terrified lighting assistant nods his head before Melissa storms off into the house. Her reaction catches the attention of the contestants who witnessed the interaction.

"Well, damn," Gerald says with a chuckle. "I can see she's not to be messed with at all."

"Yeah, you know how these Hollywood types are," David chimes in. "A whole other person when the cameras are off."

"Still, she's sexy as hell," Gerald replies with a sly grin causing Monica to frown.

"Maybe you would have a better chance at carrying her around on your back," Monica quips still upset over the competition.

The group all laugh giving Gerald a hard time as they leave the lounging area heading to various locations.

Inside the home, Chris and Tracy walk into the strategy room. It's a nice size with an all red theme with a couch a couple of coffee tables and a few flowers set up decorating the area. There is an uneasy silence between the two as Tracy avoids eye contact as much as possible. After a few moments, Chris decides to break the silence.

"So, how have you been?" He asks hoping to start a conversation with his old coworker.

"I've been fine," Tracy responds. "But you didn't bring me in here to talk about how I've been. I'm certain you're here to talk about my last day at the cell shop."

Chris chuckles as he takes a seat on the couch looking up at his old friend.

"That's my Tracy. Always to the point," he says.

"I'm not your Tracy," she snaps back. "I'm married, remember?"

"Damn it's just a saying. Take it easy," Chris responds.

"Take it easy? Take it easy?!" Tracy exclaims making Chris nervous. "I can't take it easy! I can't believe you're here right now! I'm losing my damn mind! How are you here right now?"

"The same as you. I filled out an online application," Chris calmly says as he rises from the couch noticing that his old friend is panicking.

"I... I didn't even wanna do this thing!" Tracy replies. "This was all my husband's idea! I didn't wanna do this stupid shit!"

Tracy's emotions get the best of her as tears start to stream down her face. Seeing Chris for the first time in years brought back feelings she had long thought were gone. Chris tries to calm her down as best he can.

"Hey, relax," he says while slowly approaching her. "Why are you getting so worked up about this?"

"Because... when I saw you last, I thought it would be the last time," Tracy explains while wiping her face. "I thought I wouldn't have to deal with you again. I thought I wouldn't have to-"

"Be reminded of that night?" Chris responds finishing off his old friend's words.

Tracy nods he head visually frustrated at the situation she's in.

"Look, I'm not gonna lie, it was hard seeing you after all this time too," Chris admits. "I mean that night we were together was one of the most amazing nights of my life. It took me months to get over it."

"I don't think I ever was fully over it," Tracy admits.

Chris nods his head and sighs.

"Yeah, me too," he says. "I mean I used to reach out on your Facebook page all the time hoping you'd message me back. Eventually, I realized that you don't even use that page anymore."

"No. Haven't looked at it in god knows how long," Tracy responds. "I'm sorry for acting like this. Seeing you here today just overwhelmed me with emotions that I wasn't ready for. I didn't know what to say or how to react, or even what you would say. I... I just didn't know."

"You know what I thought when I first saw you during the

reveal?" Chris says with a smirk. "I thought it must be fate that brought us together."

"Fate?" A confused Tracy responds.

"Yeah. I mean what are the odds we'd both be here right now if it wasn't fate?" Chris asks.

Tracy begins to laugh in disbelief.

"Fate? Are you serious?" She quips. "Chris, we had a fling. Once. We're both married. How can this be fate?"

"Maybe we're married to the wrong people," Chris suggests stunning Tracy. "I know, that sounds crazy, but we did what we did back then, and to be honest, I haven't been the same since then. It was only one time, true, but that one time was everything to me."

Tracy shakes her head in denial as she struggles to make sense of things.

"You say that with a child," she points out.

"Hey, my child is my child," Chris responds. "That doesn't have anything to do with this."

"It has everything to do with this," Tracy replies. "I don't know why you can't see that."

Chris takes a deep breath as he knows there is truth to what Tracy is trying to tell him. Still, he can't let go of the fact that he believes fate brought the two together that day and he didn't want to waste the time they had together.

"Trace, look, I'm not here to argue with you," he responds. "We're stuck here together. We might as well use the time we have here to figure this thing out."

"We're not stuck together anywhere," Tracy fires back as she backs away from her old friend. "I'm going to go to the producers and ask off the show. I can't believe I let my husband talk me into this."

"No, you're not," Chris responds surprising Tracy.

"Excuse me?"

"I've thought about running into you for the past two years. Ever since that night together, I wish I could... it's just now that I have you here in my presence I'm... I'm dumbfounded. Damn, I forgot how beautiful your eyes were," Chris responds gazing into Tracy's eyes.

Compliments like that are sorely missed in Tracy's marriage as hearing Chris compliment her puts a smile on her face. She remembers how Chris would make her feel beautiful each day together at the cell phone shop. She would look forward to work each day knowing that he would be there for her, and would make her feel beautiful each time they were together. Since moving to Houston, she didn't have that kind of relationship with any of her peers, and her husband could care less. That phrase about her eyes being beautiful captures her heart once more.

"Damn, I've missed you," she replies with a smile.

"I've missed you too," Chris says as he approaches her once more.

The two are silent again, as Chris takes a chance and moves into to kiss her. At the last moment, Tracy backs away leaving her old friend hanging.

"That time for us is over," she regretfully says. "What we did was nice, but we can't do it again."

"It doesn't have to be over," Chris replies. "We've been given a second chance."

"Don't make this harder than it has to be, Chris," Tracy

says as her emotions get the best of her once again. "Do I have to be the one to fight our temptation?"

"That's a burden you're putting on yourself," Chris answers. "Me, I always make it a point to follow my heart."

"Well, you have a son and a wife," Tracy again points out. "I have a husband. Do you think it's fair to follow our hearts and betray them? No matter what we had, is it worth it?"

Chris sighs as he finally backs down a bit. His heart was running wild at the moment letting his emotions blind him in regards to his family. Tracy is about to walk off when Chris calls her back.

"Hey, wait!" He says. "I mean, we do have a couple of hours here. Why don't we stay awhile and catch up? I know you threw that competition for us to talk, so what's the rush?"

"I don't know what you're talking about," Tracy replies.

"Bull shit," Chris says with a smirk. "You forget, I know you. I know everything about you, especially when you're lying."

"Yeah right," Tracy responds. "You always did think you were hot shit."

"Girl, please. I studied you from the time you were first hired," Chris explains. "I watched you eat, talk, and work. I took in any little information I could about you. I noticed you can never look anyone directly in their eyes when you're lying."

Tracy rolls her eyes and shakes her head in denial.

"I'll prove it. Look me in my eyes right now, and tell me you didn't throw that last event," Chris challenges. "Do it right now."

Tracy looks into Chris's eyes and opens her mouth to speak but nothing comes out. After a few seconds, she looks away from Chris causing him to smile knowing that he's proven his point.

"Like I said," he responds with a smirk.

"Okay, I threw the event. So what?" Quips Tracy.

"You did it knowing this is the only place we could speak freely," Chris points out. "You wanted this reunion just as bad as I did. So why are you rushing out now?"

Tracy sighs knowing Chris was right. If it would be their only time together, she figures she might as well make the best of it. After a few moments, she makes her way over towards the couch and sits with her legs crossed and her arms folded.

"Fine," she responds as if she's giving up. "So, I heard you say you are a store manager now. I assume you're talking about the old shop?"

Chris chuckles as he takes a seat next to Tracy on the couch.

"Yeah, you heard right," he answers. "Templeton got himself a call center job as a supervisor. Feel sorry for them folks for real."

Tracy chuckles remembering her old boss as the two friends put their feelings to the side and reminisce about old times.

Almost two hours later, Chris looks at the time realizing their time in the strategy room is almost up. He takes a deep breath as he gazes into Tracy's eyes once more. His look catches her attention.

"What?" She says with a smirk.

"It's almost time for us to leave," Chris replies. "It's been nice getting to hear about you these last couple of years."

"I'll admit, it was a good idea to sit here and chill," Tracy replies.

"I know, and that got me thinking that maybe we should team up and win this thing," Chris slyly responds catching Tracy off guard. "We should be teammates. We can have time like this for as long as we're on the show. What do you say?"

The once bright smile on Tracy's face starts to fade.

"I don't think that's a good idea," she answers. "Look, this was nice, but I don't know about all that. You convinced me to stay, and I'll do that, but me and you together... in this place? What if we become weak again?"

"Then we do what fate wants us to do," Chris replies causing Tracy to giggle.

"Here you go with that fate shit again," she says. "I just think the more we keep apart the better things will be."

"Well, it's not your choice is it," Chris responds as he rises from the couch. "It is man's week, so there's nothing you can do about it."

"Chris, I'm serious! Don't do this," Tracy pleads with him.

Chris smiles as he quickly makes his way out of the strategy room. Tracy sits on the couch in disbelief as she wonders if Chris would follow through with his threat of adding her to his team. She didn't want their closeness to show on camera, or her husband to recognize Chris. She even wondered if Chris's wife recognized her on the show. They've only met once at Chris's wedding, but as a woman, she knows any woman in a relationship remembers all friendly females in their man's life. She sighs as she thinks for a few moments to herself before finally making her way out of the strategy room.

Later that night, Dunbar is reviewing the show taking notes from his spacious living room area as he rewinds the show back and forth judging everything from the lighting to Melissa's performance as a host. After taking several notes he starts to rewind the moment of the competition where Tracy fell off of Mitch's back. He's not buying her performance thinking that she purposely staged the event. After several reviews, his cell phone begins to ring. He pauses the show before answering the line knowing that it's Margie calling.

"Yeah, what do you have?" He answers.

"Hey. I just got the ratings report back on today's episode, and sir... well it's not that good," Margie responds causing Dunbar to cringe.

"Well, what do they expect?" A frustrated Dunbar responds. "I mean with that stupid game?! I could have come up with something better than that!"

"Well, be that as it may, if it keeps going this way, we'll be out on our you know what, sir," Margie responds causing Dunbar to grab his head.

"Right. Did you do what I asked, about the background checks?" He asks his assistant.

"Yes, sir. It'll be back in a couple of days," Margie answers. "Nothing really to report after hours so far, but some of the crew said they think that Chris and Tracy may have known each other outside of the show."

Dunbar perks up after hearing the news.

"Really? What makes them think that?" He asks.

"Nothing specific, but they just seem to have a vibe like they've met before. Looks and avoidance at times. I watched some of the after hour videos and I didn't see much but they would know more about it than me."

"Interesting," Dunbar responds as he leans back in his chair. "That might be an angle we can play on. Didn't those two talk in the strategy room earlier?"

"Yeah, so?"

"Have the editors send me a copy of that conversation," Dunbar orders which confuses Margie.

"How? The strategy room doesn't have cameras," Margie replies.

"Yes it does," Dunbar points out. "For insurance purposes, we were forced to put in cameras in every room after season four just in case. That was the season that Gloria claimed her teammate Brian sexually abused her in the strategy room. We've been in and out of court over that since then so cameras were put in to avoid just that."

"Oh, yeah. I totally forgot about that. I didn't know cameras were put it though," Margie responds. "Still it's deceiving to use that footage for anything other than a lawsuit. All the contestants are under the impression that the room is camera free."

"Just get them to send me the damn footage!" Dunbar snaps back. "This could be the beginning of something for us. In the meantime, make sure those two interact with each other as much as possible. Also, assign a cameraman to follow on those two. The kind they don't see."

"You want me to fix the show?" Margie asks for confirmation.

"Yes! Do I have to spell it out for you?!" Dunbar fires back. "I want you to fix the damn show! The more we have those two interacting the more dirt we may find! We're hanging on by a thread here and need something to run with!"

"Sir, I really think you should run this by Mr. Brooks," Margie warns. "I mean we could be opening up-"

"Margie, let me make this as clear as I can. Either you make this happen, or I'll find someone else who can. Are we clear?" A threatening Dunbar responds.

"Crystal, sir," Margie responds.

"Good. Now get it done," Dunbar responds before hanging up the line.

He calms himself down before starting the show's video again watching as Tracy falls off of Mitch. A wicked grin fills his face thinking of the different ways he can twist the narrative.

At the Team Experiment house, late night, the weather is perfect with a slight breeze flowing through the outside area on occasion. Monica, Lucia, and Julia are sitting outside at the lounging area gawking at Victoria who is wearing a skimpy two-piece bikini poolside hanging with the males of the group. She's getting real touchy-feely with some of the men causing the trio to judge her from a distance.

"You see, that's some bull shit right there," Lucia says before taking a sip of her drink.

"I mean, they do know this is a nationally televised show don't they?" Julia asks. "I can't believe she is just all over them like that. Seriously, what married woman does that?"

"Somebody who hasn't been married that long and is still living that single lifestyle," Monica says. "I know one thing. If that was my man, I'd be waiting outside of this house ready to beat her ass."

"It's just disgusting, I mean look at that," Lucia replies as she points out Victoria whispering something into Mitch's ear as the two share a secret with each other.

They both laugh which sickens the ladies once more. As the judgmental trio continues to watch Victoria seducing the men around her, Tracy walks out of the house and makes her way over to the lounge area as well.

"Hey, everyone. What's going on?" She asks as she takes a seat.

"Nothing, just watching slutzilla over there sharing her goodies with the guys," Lucia responds, turning Tracy's attention to the poolside.

Tracy is surprised to watch Victoria flirting with all the male contestants. She notices Chris is sitting at the far end of the poolside, not really saying much.

"I know girls like that. Most of the time it's an attention thing. They love to be the center of it all," Tracy responds. "It's not a big deal."

"So, you're telling me you wouldn't have a problem with your husband in another woman's face like that?" Julia asks her. "Cause that wouldn't work for me."

"Hell naw! That's just disrespectful. And she's supposed to be married?! Seriously?!" A worked up, Lucia, says as she continues to watch Victoria's antics.

"You have to understand, she's young and newly married," Tracy points out. "She may not have gotten all that single shit out her. Either that or... or maybe she's with a guy that doesn't show her any attention and this is a way to get what she doesn't get at home."

As Tracy reflects on her own marriage, she and the others watch as Victoria gets into the pool and swims up to Chris, who is sitting poolside with his feet in the water. She makes her way between his legs and leans in with a smile. After a few words,

Chris begins to chuckle, which upsets Tracy.

"Or maybe you're right, and she's just a hoe," she fires back, causing the others to giggle.

"So, Ms. Tracy, how did your meeting go with my man?" Julia asks with a smirk.

"Yeah, chica, what happened? What did y'all talk about?" Lucia asks as all eyes are now on Tracy.

"Nothing really. Just asked about me and my background. We talked about life outside of here. Nothing special," Tracy replies, trying to hide the details of their meeting.

"Well, I hope you didn't sweet talk him away from me," Julia responds. "I don't mind being partnered with someone with his certain set of skills."

Julia gives Chris a look admiring his smile from a distance.

"Yeah, I think I can get far with him," she says when everyone suddenly looks at her.

Julia's embarrassed as she starts to giggle.

"I mean in the competition," she clarifies as she turns red.

"Sure, that's what you meant," Lucia responds. "I like my partner. Don't get me wrong; he doesn't have those abs like Chris and Mitch, but he's kind of cute and don't take this the wrong way, Julia, but I'm normally not into white guys. So if I'm giving him credit, he must be fine!"

All the ladies giggle, even managing to get a smirk from Tracy.

"Well, baby, it seems I got the runt of the litter," Monica says, referring to Gerald. "I mean he ain't nothing but skin and bones. I know I'm thick and all, but that poor child couldn't get me to the pool once. I hope he can at least help with the trivia portion. If he's weak and dumb, I'm probably gonna be the first one out of here."

"I don't know, he's skinny, but sometimes that's all you need. Helps with that good feeling, if you know what I mean," Julia says with a giggle.

Tracy is in disbelief as the ladies continue to chatter about the men.

"Ladies, I mean weren't we just talking about how Victoria is out there flirting with the guys, and we're over here subjecting them to the same thing?" Tracy asks.

"No, mami. You see we're just having a little girl talk," Lucia replies. "She's out there flinging herself around. It's different."

"Yeah, Tracy. Sista to sista, you know how we get down," Monica says. "A little girl talk never hurt anybody."

"Yeah. Loosen up a bit. There's some wine coolers in the fridge," Julia says. "We're in California with the breeze flowing through our hair, some sexy men to look at, and the perfect weather to just hang out in. I can only imagine how hot it is back in Amarillo."

"Who you telling? Hell, even if I am the first one bounced out of here, it'll be worth it for the two-week vacation," Monica responds as she and Julia toast their glasses.

The conversation continues as the ladies move on to other topics. Tracy glances every so often to catch a glimpse of Victoria and Chris interacting with each other. She can't believe he's entertaining her. Her disdain continues to grow with every glimpse she gets of the two.

Chapter 6

Truth and Laughter

A few days have gone by since the first competition. Chris has met with all the female contestants except Victoria, who he is scheduled to meet in a few minutes. It's been a calm few days with everyone getting to know each other better. Their living quarters are shared, and most have gotten used to sharing their area with only a few brushes ups on the women's side. Chris and Tracy stayed away from each other for the most part, trying to keep their relationship a secret from the others, but the feelings the two shared for one another is making it harder to conceal. Chris is leaning on the wall next to the strategy, seemingly exhausted as he's struggling to sleep ever since coming to the house. Victoria makes her way towards Chris with a sexy sway in her walk with her now traditional scantily dressed attire and a big smile on her face.

"Hey. So I see you saved the best for last," she says as she pokes Chris in the stomach, causing him to chuckle.

"I guess I did," Chris replies before opening the door to the strategy room. "Shall we?"

Victoria smiles as she enters the room, followed by Chris. She takes a seat on the couch, crosses her legs, and waits for

Chris to join her. He decides to stand as Victoria makes him a little nervous with her aggressive ways.

"So, I guess we're here to talk about what it would be like if we teamed up," Chris says, trying to hurry the meeting as fast as he can.

"We could, or we can do a few other things," Victoria replies with a smirk.

Chris catches on to what she's hinting at and begins to chuckle nervously.

"Victoria, I was under the impression that all the folks here were married. Yet, and this is no disrespect or anything, but you don't carry yourself as a married person," he replies.

Victoria giggles and shakes her head.

"I guess everyone's out there talking about me, aren't they?" She replies.

"Well, I mean it is a little strange, that's all," Chris answers. "I can't speak for others, but I know I've been thinking about it. What's up with that?"

Victoria's once bright smile starts to falter a bit.

"I get it. I understand how things can be interpreted. Look, I just like to have a little fun, that's all. Besides, I plan on having a career after this show one way or another," Victoria admits. "Reality TV is a big business, and if I get picked up because of what I do here, whether I win or not, I'll be set up for life."

Chris nods his head finally understanding the persona Victoria was portraying.

"So you telling me all this, all the flirting, the outfits, that's all for show?" He asks.

Victoria giggles as she rises from the couch and approaches Chris seductively.

"Well, not all," she answers while looking Chris up and down. "Like I told you poolside that night, I wouldn't mind teaming up with you. Get a little more time in this room weekly. It doesn't always have to be about the game. We can see what happens and go from there. So what do you think?"

Chris looks on nervously once more as Victoria invades his space. As she looks at him, she realizes that he's not interested at all in her, which she found odd. She had all the men's attention in the game and was stunned Chris wasn't buying in. She had her thoughts on why, however.

"I see," she says before backing down. "You've already made up your mind. It was never going to be me. You have eyes only for one."

Chris is confused as he scratches his head.

"What are you talking about?" He asks.

"Don't play dumb, Chris. It's all about you and Tracy. You'd have to be blind not to see it."

"I... I... I don't know what you're talking about," Chris stutters.

"Oh, yeah, that answer sounds like the truth," a sarcastic Victoria responds with a smirk. "Look, I know I'm not going to be able to outduel her. Maybe the others don't see it, but I can tell. All the awkward looks, and how you two try and not speak with each other when we gather. I mean, it's crazy if you think about it. If you two want to hide it, that's fine. I don't know what you and her have going on, but my lips are sealed. All I'm saying is that maybe me and you can work together even if we're not on the same team. Help me sell the storyline or something like that. At the end of the day, it's all reality, and reality is fake."

Chris chuckles, hearing Victoria's plan.

"Sure, why not," he responds. "Whatever you need to get to your reality, celebrity goal."

"Great. I'll try and throw you signs when I can. Whatever we can do, argument, playful things, flirting, or whatever works for the moment, we can do," an excited Victoria says. "We can play off each other. It'll be fun, you'll see!"

Chris nods his head as Victoria approaches him once again, making sure her body is pressed against his.

"Now that all of that is out the way, I wasn't kidding about doing other things," she said with a smirk. "You may not get another chance. This tongue on your chest working its way down your body. Isn't that something you'd like to experience?"

She blows slightly in Chris's ear before running her tongue on his lobe. Chris is excited. Nothing would please him more than taking Victoria in that room. He decides against it as he backs away from Victoria, rejecting her advances.

"Trust me, if this was before marriage, I wouldn't hesitate," he explains to Victoria before giving her body a quick look. "But be that as it may, I'm going to have to pass."

Victoria nods her head and smiles once again before heading towards the exit.

"Have it your way," she quips before making it out of the room.

Chris breathes a sigh of relief before looking down and notices his full-blown erection.

"Jesus Christ," he says to himself with a chuckle.

He decides to wait a moment until his erection dies down to avoid embarrassment. Unfortunately for him, it's a long-lasting erection which would require patience.

A little over an hour later, all the contestants meet outside once again, prepping for the next competition. Chris and Julia are standing at the far end when Tracy looks over towards Chris with an attitude. She is still upset with his poolside manner a few nights ago with Victoria. She knows the two just had a meeting in the strategy room earlier that day. She looks over towards Victoria as well, who is all over David flirting away. The females were told to arrive barefoot with shorts on, but as always, Victoria took things to the limit. She had her booty shorts on, attracting attention from the male contestants and crew members as she struts her way around the yard with her arm wrapped around David. It sickens Tracy to see that. Not that she cares about David, but how Victoria was carrying herself with all her male counterparts, especially Chris. Mitch notice's his partner's mood and tries to snap her out of the funk.

"Hey, you alright?" He asks.

"Yeah. I'm fine," she replies.

"Alright, cool. I need your head in the game. We need to make our move today if we're gonna win this thing," Mitch says, trying to hype his partner up.

"You're right. Today is the day," Tracy responds with a smirk as the two partners dap each other off.

The crew staff lets the contestants know it's time to line up as they all pair with their partners waiting for the broadcast to start. They all notice a table with restraints attached in the middle of the yard and are curious about what will happen with the next event. Victoria giggles at the chair as it reminds her of a BSDM device. Melissa makes her way outside of the house barking orders to her assistant walking side-by-side with her before running off to carry out her boss's orders. After a few moments, Melissa turns on the charm and smiles as the camera begins counting down.

"Welcome to today's edition of Team Experiment! I'm your host, Melissa, and we're going to start off today's show with a little competition that's all about laughter!" She says, confusing the contestants. "Ladies, we're about to start the show off testing your threshold today."

Melissa walks over towards the table as everyone looks on.

"Over here, ladies, we have our table of restraint. Each of you will have your turn on the table as you will be tortured by a rival male from another team," she says with glee as Tracy and the other females all look worried.

Melissa begins laughing after noticing their expressions.

"I see you ladies are concerned," she says with a smirk. "Don't worry, we're beyond medieval times here. According to your profiles, all of you are extremely ticklish. Knowing that, we decided to take advantage of that today with our extreme tickle challenge!"

The female contestant's faces don't change much as each of them seems worried about what's in store for them.

"You will be tied and tickled by one male from a rival team. The male who gets their victim to submit the quickest gets one hundred points for their team. Second place will get you seventy five points, third place fifty points, and the bottom two finishers will net your women nothing but smiles," Melissa explains to the contestants. "Men, you're allowed to tickle any-where from the neck up, stomach, knees, underarms, and feet. The clock starts as soon as you touch your victim and ends once she submits. If there is a tie for first, we would go to a tickle off to determine a winner. We've already paired off everyone, so fellas, get ready, and to the ladies, good luck. We'll be back with extreme tickling right after these messages."

The cameraman yells clear as Melissa looks at her card for the pairings.

"Okay, Mitch, your victim will be Julia in this event. Chris, you have Tracy, David, you have Victoria, Sebastian, you take Monica, and Gerald, you have Lucia," she informs the contestants. "Now please, remember we're on live TV, so don't do anything crazy during this event. Good luck."

Melissa walks over to the makeup artist to get touched up as Tracy drops her head after hearing Chris is the one who will torment her. She's about to approach Chris when Julia cuts her off, looking nervously at her partner.

"Chris, I... I can't do this," she says with a stutter. "I don't think I can last long, for real! I'm like really ticklish! Like really bad! Especially on my-"

"Wait! Don't say it out loud," Chris says as he pulls Julia to the side. "Look, don't sweat it. Just hold out as long as you can. I'll take care of things on my end."

Julia nods her head, but Chris's words don't give her any comfort as she walks off nervously. Tracy finally makes her way over to Chris after eavesdropping on their conversation.

"So, you think you got it like that?" She says, catching his attention.

"Excuse me?"

"You're over here talking like you already got this thing won. I'm just saying," Tracy responds. "I know you're disappointed you can't put your hands on Victoria though. If you already haven't anyway."

"What's that supposed to mean?" A confused Chris asks.

"It means exactly what I said it means," Tracy quips back before noticing the contestants are getting ready for the return of the commercial break.

Chris jogs into place as the paring of Gerald and Lucia are already in position, with Lucia strapped tightly on top of the table. Gerald looks confident as he checks out the beautiful Hispanic rival.

"Do me a favor, and make this quick," he says, playing mind games with her. "I don't want to have to break you, but I will."

"Ha, bring it, skinny boy," Lucia fires back. "You not getting anywhere with me."

Gerald nods his head, loving the challenge as the countdown to return live starts. Melissa joins the duo by the table as she looks into the camera with her legendary smile.

"Welcome back. As you can see, we're all set up with our first competitors Gerald and Lucia. Gerald, is there anything you'd like to say to your victim before we get started?"

"Yes there is, Melissa," Gerald responds before turning his attention towards his rival. "Lucia, I'm giving you one last chance to tap out now. Save yourself some laughter."

Lucia giggles as she's amused by Gerald's threats.

"Bring it!" She exclaims.

"Alright. Well, good luck to both of you. Gerald, the timer begins as soon as you touch her," Melissa says before backing away from the camera frame.

Gerald wastes little time as he begins tickling Lucia under her exposed arms. Lucia has no defense with her wrists strapped above her head and begins laughing profusely, unable to avoid Gerald's touch. After several moments of tormenting her armpits, Monica begins instructing her partner from the sideline.

"Come on, Gerald! Get her feet! Her feet!" Monica yells,

grabbing her partner's attention.

Gerald does as he's instructed as he begins to tickling Lucia's feet, causing her to jerk on the restraints. The torment is too much as Lucia finally gives in, lasting about two and a half minutes. David runs over and releases his partner from her restraints as Melissa walks back over towards the table.

"Two minutes and thirty seconds. Not bad, Lucia," she says to Lucia, who is still giggling after the onslaught.

She's helped to the sideline by David when Melissa turns her attention towards Victoria.

"Victoria, Lucia set a pretty impressive time. Think you're up to the challenge?" She asks.

Victoria sways her way over and smiles. She shows her sex appeal to the camera before lying down on the table, awaiting to get strapped in.

"Just another day for me," she responds, alluding to the fact that's she's comfortable with bondage.

Back at the studio headquarters, the show is playing in the background on a TV in Dunbar's office showing Victoria being tickled by David. However, Dunbar's attention is glued to his computer as he's finally received the footage from Chris and Tracy's strategy room meeting from a few days ago. He's in absolute shock listening to the discussion they had about their affair. Each word coming out of their mouths excites him even more. After the video ends, he leans back in his seat still processing what he has just heard. He quickly grabs his phone and dials Margie.

"Margie, where are you?" He asks as soon as she picks up. "Well, I don't need you at the house. I need you back at the office, now. I've found something that's going to give us the ratings boost we're looking for."

He quickly hangs up the phone and chuckles to himself ready to unleash Chris and Tracy's secret to the world.

Back at the Team Experiment House, Monica has just finished her torment as Sebastian made her submit in about a minute and a half, which puts him and Victoria's team in the lead. Gerald and Monica are in second place, and due to Victoria holding out for over three minutes, David and Lucia's team are currently in last place. Up next is Julia, who is still extremely nervous. Tracy looks over and notices Julia rubbing on the back of her knees. She smiles as she whispers to her partner, Mitch.

"This should be easy. Hit the back of her knees," Tracy instructs to a confused Mitch.

"The back of her knees? Come on. My plan is to start at her feet," Mitch replies. "Why would I hit her knees?"

"Because she's over there trying to hide her spot. Look," Tracy says as she turns her attention to Julia.

Before Julia hops on the table, she grabs the back of her knees once more, which surprises Mitch.

"Could be a game she's playing," Mitch responds. "Maybe trying to get me to attack her knees while hiding her real spot. I could waste a lot of time if that's the case."

"Trust me, she did that as a reaction. Hit the knees, and hit them hard," Tracy commands, surprising Mitch.

After a few moments, he nods his head.

"You better be right about this," he says.

"Trust me. She's going to break quick," Tracy responds with a smirk.

By the table, Julia is getting strapped in and is a nervous wreck. Chris is standing next to her, trying to keep her calm.

"Chris... I... I don't know," Julia responds as her ankles are strapped on the table.

"Listen to me, Julia, you got this," Chris responds. "Just give me thirty seconds. Can you do that? I can beat it, but I need at least thirty seconds."

"Thirty seconds?" Julia questions.

"That's all I need. Can you do that for me?" Chris asks.

Julia thinks for a moment before slowly nodding her head.

"I can do thirty seconds," she responds.

Chris smiles and taps her on the ankle before walking off. Mitch walks over with a smile on his face making Julia feel very nervous. Melissa joins the two and turns her attention towards Mitch.

"Mitch, any last words for your victim Julia here?" She asks.

"Yeah, I just hope those knees of hers aren't ticklish," Mitch responds, sending shocks down Julia's spine.

"Julia, anything you'd like to say to your tormentor?" Melissa asks.

Julia doesn't say a word as Melissa looks on curiously.

"Interesting. Well, you know the routine. The clock starts at first touch. Good luck to the both of you," Melissa responds before moving out of the camera frame.

Mitch waste no time going for the back of Julia's knees, which sends her to a state of laughter unseen thus far in the competition. She begins bucking trying to fight her way free but is unable to block her most sensitive spot.

"Come on, Julia!" Chris shouts. "Fight it! Fight it! Don't let him beat you!"

"Hit her faster!" Tracy shouts to Mitch, catching Chris off guard. "She's about to break!"

Mitch begins stroking Julia's hind knees much faster, causing the blonde to tap out.

"Wow, twenty-six seconds!" Melissa says as she walks back over to the table. "I think we may have found the most ticklish girl on the planet! Way to go, Mitch! You have taken the lead with that performance."

Chris walks over and helps unfasten his partner from the table when he glances over and notices Mitch and Tracy celebrating. He and Tracy's eyes meet, causing Tracy to stick her tongue out at her old friend. Chris nods his head at her before turning his attention back to Julia, who looks as though she's been through war.

"I'm sorry, Chris. I let you down," she says, still trying to catch her breath.

"Don't sweat it. You did what I needed you to do," Chris replies with a reassuring smile.

"Chris, I broke in twenty-six seconds," Julia reminds him as she hops off the table. "You would have to break her faster than that. What can you possibly do to beat that time?"

"I have it under control," Chris replies as he heads back to the table where Tracy is now getting strapped in.

He has a look of confidence in his eyes watching his old lover being restrained. Once she's fully strapped in, Melissa makes her way over to do the pre-competition interview.

"Chris, you're going to have to get Tracy to submit in

under twenty-six seconds to win the hundred points, which is going to be a tough mark to beat. Any words to your victim before you get started?" Melissa asks.

"Yeah. You stuck your tongue out at me just a second ago. Bad decision," he says to Tracy with a smirk.

"Tracy, your responds?" Melissa says.

"I have one thing to say," Tracy replies before sticking her tongue out at Chris one more.

"Well, these two seem to be ready. Ok, Chris, as usual, the time will start as soon as you touch her. Good luck," Melissa says before scurrying off.

Chris slowly circles Tracy as if he's stalking her, making everyone watching curiously as to what he's doing. Tracy tries to turn her head to keep up with Chris wondering what he's up to as well. Mitch and Julia are cheering for their teammates as the entire household, and the nation waits for Chris to make his move. After a few moments, Chris positions himself right above Tracy's head. He gently begins stroking her ears, causing Tracy to scream out and submit quickly. The household contestants are stunned as Julia runs over to celebrate with her partner. Melissa is in disbelief as well as she makes her way over to Chris for the post-competition interview.

"Unbelievable!" She says with a smile. "Three seconds. That has to be a record somewhere. Chris, I have to ask, but what made you pick that specific spot to attack?"

Chris chuckles nervously trying to come up with a good excuse to explain the vast knowledge of Tracy's weak spot.

"Well... what made me pick that spot is... well, I was just going to start from the top and work my way down. That was my strategy going into this, so... I guess I just got lucky," Chris responds, trying to convince Melissa, the contestants, and the viewers at home.

"Well, luck has given you and Julia a monster lead with an extra one hundred points bringing your total to two hundred points. Mitch and Tracy hit the board with seventy-five points, and Sebastian and Victoria in third place with fifty points. Team's two and three better get their act together before the others run away with this thing. On the next episode, the competition heats up as we will also have Chris's decision! Will he swap partners with a huge lead? Find out this Friday on the next episode of Team Experiment."

The contestants clap as Tracy is helped up from the table by Mitch. She glances over towards Chris, who sticks his tongue out playfully, causing her to chuckle to herself. She couldn't believe that Chris would do that to her on national TV. Mitch is consoling her as the contestants all head back in the house after the show is off the air.

Back at the studio headquarters, Dunbar is checking out the polls for the latest episode with a smirk as the numbers are higher than the previous episode. He also checks out the contestant ratings, which gives him insight on how likable each contestant is. He's excited about everything going on when Margie makes her way into his office, holding a few files with her.

"Sir, we have a problem," she says before Dunbar shushes her.

"Margie, I'm taking a look at the numbers here, and it seems like we had a monster showing on that last episode," he says with glee. "So far we're tracking over a three hundred percent uptick in viewership! I spoke to Mr. Brooks earlier, and he was impressed as well! Margie, I think we may have got something here!"

"That's great, sir. But I think you better-"

"Wait! There's more!" Dunbar says, cutting off his assistant. "I had a poll run on each of the contestants' likability, and I bet you can guess on who had the top two scores!"

"Well, yeah, I probably could," Margie says, hoping to get a word in. "The thing is, under the circumstances we-"

"Shut up for a second, Margie," Dunbar says before continuing. "If you were thinking the top two contestants were Chris and Tracy, you'd be absolutely correct. America is in love with these two, and do you know why?"

"Sir, please. If you just listen to me, I can-"

"I don't want to hear the end of any sentences!" Dunbar says as he leans back in his chair. "I saw the strategy room footage, finally. Not only did these two know each other on the outside, but they also had an affair! Isn't that wonderful? These two are just what we need! They're hot, they're sexy, they're-"

"About to get kicked off the show!" Margie exclaims, finally getting a word in.

Dunbar looks at her as if he's offended.

"Why would we kick off our highest-rated contestants?" He asks.

"Sir, with all due respect, we can't have this on the show," Margie answers. "If word of this leaks out, we'll be ruined. It's not the type of filth we want to associate with the show."

"Bullshit! It's exactly what we need," Dunbar says as he approaches his assistant. "And who needs to leak it out when we can play on it. Let America in on the secret. It'll be a real live Truman Show!"

Margie grabs her head out of frustration before addressing her boss.

"Besides the obvious moral issue here, there's also the

issue of the legal ramifications that this will cause," Margie explains. "Do you really think that their spouses are going to let us embarrass them like that?"

"You forget, we are the showrunners. They signed a release form that anything filmed in the house is our property, and that includes the strategy room footage," Dunbar reminds his assistant. "It's ours to do with as we please. I do like this whole leaked angle though, now that I think about it. Some way we build it up to a reveal show! Then we can have a segment called "Strategy Files" where we'll release this plus other team's discussions! This will be huge!"

"Sir! These people are married!" Margie exclaims. "You can't do this! It'll ruin their lives!"

"All's fair in love and ratings, Margie," Dunbar says as he takes a seat back behind his desk. "It's nothing personal. It's just business. To each his own."

"Enough of the clichés! This is serious!" Marie reiterates. "You're turning a family-friendly show into some cheap reality show stunt. That's not why we're here! Sir, please, you can't do this."

"Margie, if you don't want to be involved, I totally understand," Dunbar responds as he unlocks his computer. "Like I always say, I can find someone else to do what needs to be done if you don't have the stomach for it."

Margie sighs because she knew this was coming. Dunbar might be low on the WBC Studio totem pole, but his name still rings out in Hollywood in certain circles, which is why she started working for him in the first place. She wanted to be a producer herself one day, and working with Dunbar will give her the experience she needs to get to where she wants in her career. If she was to leave or get fired by Dunbar, it would be a mark that sets her back by years. As strongly as she feels about revealing Chris and Tracy's relationship to the world, her hands are tied.

"Fine," she responds with attitude. "But let me be clear, I'm against this whole thing. I think this is going to blow up in our faces."

"Noted, now get the editors on board with what's going on, and have them put something together. I want a plan mapped out on not only how we're going to make sure these two remain on the show, but storylines and selling this relationship to the public," Dunbar tells an unenthused Margie. "Oh, and by the way, we have to make sure the contestants don't get wind of this. I would assume that goes without saying."

Margie sighs with a frown on her face before nodding her head. She quickly makes her way out of her boss's office to execute his orders. Dunbar leans back in his chair with a cryptic smile on his face as he looks over the numbers once again dreaming of what's to come.

Chapter 7

Other Than Our Spouses

A couple of days after their last competition, the male contestants have surrendered the living room area to the females so they can watch a couple of romantic comedies together. With the living room occupied with emotions, the men decide to gather outside in the lounge area for a late-night guy's night out. Unbeknownst to them, the show has started a buildup about a secret love affair two of the contestants have had in the past. The interest has spiked viewership and has everyone wondering who the two contestants have a secret to hide. Chris and the others are laughing and enjoying a beer finally able to relax. David lights a cigarette and offers one to the others in the group, who all refuse.

"No smokers in the crowd I see," he says before taking a puff.

"Nah, those things will kill you," Sebastian remarks.

"We're all gonna die, my friend. Might as well enjoy life while we can," David responds.

"I guess that's one way to look at it," Sebastian says.

"The surgeon general can say what he wants, but cigarettes are a necessity, especially after sex," David jokes with a chuckle.

"I'll agree with that," Gerald chimes in. "I've been off the tobacco for about a year now, and I'm good for the most part. The one thing where I'm tempted the most is after sex. Hell, it's almost as good as the sex at times."

All the men laugh as Chris shakes his head in denial.

"Okay, first of all, you're too young to make that statement," Chris says. "Secondly, there's nothing better than the love of a good woman. No cigarette or anything else can duplicate that feeling."

"I will give you that," Mitch responds before taking a sip of his beer. "A good woman can get you through some tough times. Especially when the world is grabbing you by the balls. That release after a frustrating day... let me say there's nothing like it."

"I disagree," Sebastian quips. "Sex is just sex. I don't believe there's such a thing as bad sex and good sex."

"Speak for yourself," David fires back. "There's certain levels to sex, and I've had them all. You can't tell me different. In fact, let me blow your mind. The best sex I ever had was-"

"Let me just remind you that the cameras are running twenty-four-seven here," Chris warns catching David off guard.

"Was with my loving wife," David quickly finishes causing the group to laugh at him.

"Alright, let's just say for the sake of argument that the best sex we all had was with our wives, agreed?" Chris announces.

All the men shake their heads as Chris turns back towards

David.

"Alright, you were saying?" He said with a grin.

"Right, well, other than my wife, the best sex I ever had was with young stewardess back in my college days," David continues. "This was a girl who sexy as hell and knew her way around the bedroom. When she would land, we'd meet up at my dorm, have a few drinks, and before I know it, she would throw that thing on me that would have me in tears! I shit you not."

"Did you make her wear the uniform?" Sebastian inquires, causing the others to chuckle.

"Hell yeah," David boasts. "I don't know. It's something about stewardesses that's so damn attractive. The airlines know what they're doing when they hire these women. I mean, think about it. Other than the guys working there, when was the last time you've seen an ugly stewardess? Even the Milfs are cute as hell. Talk about discrimination."

Chris takes a sip of his beer as Mitch decides to share his story.

"Speaking of stewardesses, the best sex I've had, other than my wife, of course, is with this lovely thing I met on a trip out in New York," he explains. "When I was younger, I always wanted to live in NYC. The big lights, the money, the hustle; it was all a drug to me, and I was addicted to it. As you may know, with all that comes the big bills, the high rent, and struggle. I was at this bar one night, not too far from where all the Wall Street execs like to hang out, when I ran into this trader named Melissa. She was working on getting her broker's license. She was in town from Colorado trying to take in the scene and working an internship or something."

Mitch takes a quick swig of his drinking before continuing the story.

"Anyway, long story short, while she was there, me and her dated for about a month until it was time for her internship to end. She invited me to come take a trip back down to Colorado for a few days so we could hang out a little bit longer before she started school back. Now, this girl is loaded. Well, her family was. Anyway, she said she'd pay for the whole trip. I was like fuck it, why not," he continues, smirking while reminiscing on the event. "I'm talking first class and everything. While we were on the plane, we were snuggled up under a blanket when she reaches down, goes into my pants, and starts playing with my shit."

The other men are hanging off Mitch's every word as he continues with his story.

"I'm looking around all nervous when she tells me she wants me inside of her right then and there. I'm like, what in the hell is going on here," he chuckles. "So she leads me into the bathroom, and that's where I officially became a member of the mile-high club."

Chris and the others are amazed, except for Gerald, who looks on confused.

"I don't get it," Gerald responds. "What's a mile high club?"

"It's when you have sex on an airplane, while in flight," Mitch responds. "They don't teach you youngsters this type of stuff anymore?"

"I've never heard of it," Gerald replies. "Those bathrooms are tight as hell. How were both of you able to fit in there, let alone have sex?"

"Well, that's the thing. Back in those days, the bathrooms were a little bigger than what they have today," Mitch describes. "And also, in first class, the bathrooms are a lot bigger. It was still a tight fit, but we pulled it off. I don't know if it was the cabin pressure, the altitude, or what, but the orgasm you feel having sex up in the air was amazing! I don't remember ever feeling like that again. Just fucking awesome, my friends."

The group all converse with each other for a moment in awe with Mitch's story. As they laugh and joke, Gerald interrupts the group to tell his tale of old sexual escapades.

"Alright, from NY to LA," he starts off with a smirk. "I met this badass chick down in Santa Monica Beach. It was crazy how we met. I'm hanging with a few of my friends, and they decided to go swimming in the water. I don't know how to swim, so I hang back and chill and watch over everyone's stuff, you know. So here I am, on the beach enjoying the perfect weather much like we are today, and who trips and falls on me? The girl of my dreams."

Gerald smiles as he thinks about the moment that changed his life.

"She was drop-dead gorgeous. I don't know if she was trying to avoid something in the sand or what, but she trips over and literally falls on top of me," he says. "We laughed about it, and we got to talking, and after a while, I finally built up the courage to ask Natalie out."

"Damn, man, chill out with the names," Chris warns. "TV cameras? Remember?"

"Right, my fault," apologizes Gerald before he continues. "So, me and her went out a couple of times before she finally invited me over to her apartment. This girl had a nightstand of pleasure or something she called it. I'm talking about any type of kink you desired, she had a tool for it. She acted all shy initially, but once we got in the bed, I could tell she was a pro. She worked me so good that I promised you, I must have busted a load at least five times that night. I never had that many orgasms in my life, and haven't since then. Hell, I didn't think it was scientifically possible. When we were done, I damn near proposed to her. I mean, she will always be the greatest sex I ever had... other than the wife of course."

"What did you say her name was again?" Mitch jokes, getting a laugh out of the others. "Cause I gotta ask if the sex was that good, what happened? Maybe I can pay her a visit while we're out here."

Gerald chuckles for a moment when the smile slowly started to fade from his face.

"Well, you'd have to visit her in the morgue," he replies, stunning the others. "Heard someone killed her last month. Stabbed her in her apartment. She wasn't wound too tightly, as I found out later. She would just spazz off for no reason sometimes. It goes to show you, sex isn't everything, no matter what we think."

Chris and the others nod as the attention is turned towards Sebastian.

"Alright, Sebass, out with it," Mitch says. "What's the best sex you ever had?"

"I just told you, sex is just sex to me," Sebastian re-iterates. "I've been with plenty of women, and to me, it's just a way to release. Nothing special."

"Bullshit," David challenges. "You can't tell me there hasn't been a single woman that you've ever had sex with that didn't get you talking in tongues, or caught you off guard."

Sebastian has a look on his face that David catches.

"That face! Right there!" He exclaims. "Who was it you were thinking about just at that moment?"

Sebastian laughs, knowing his face betrayed him.

"Alright, alright. Look, it was actually my first time," he

admits. "I mean, I knew what sex was, but I didn't know what it would feel like, you know. All the porn and stuff I used to watch with my friends where we would lie about having sex with girls we had gone to school with, it never prepared me for my first encounter."

"Alright, now we're getting somewhere. So spill it, Sebass. Let's hear about it," Mitch says as the group all await Sebastian's story.

"I had just turned eighteen, and I was determined to finally see what sex was about," Sebastian tells the group. "I had just graduated from high school, and I was about to go to college in the fall, which had me wanting pop that cherry finally. A friend of mine was having this graduation party, and I was drunk out of my mind. His parents were out of town, and he decided to get us some booze, which also was a first for me. I ran into this classmate of mine who I always had liked, but was too shy to approach her. Well, the beer made me a new man, because I went right up to her, told her how I felt, and what my intentions were, which is to lay with her before the night ended."

The others chuckled, listening to Sebastian's story.

"Yeah, the alcohol will do that to you," Mitch chimes in. "So, how did she take it?"

"She was a little surprised by it, saying that I was always so quiet in school, and she never heard me talk like that," Sebastian answers. "Needless to say, she was down. I snuck up to my friend's parent's room and locked the door. Dude, I didn't even know what the hell I was doing, and I don't think she knew either. I don't remember if it was her first time or not. All I remember was when I inserted myself, it was the warmest feeling. It caught me off guard. So much so that maybe about five pumps in, I had my first orgasm. I didn't know what the hell had happened, but I never felt anything like it before. Well, maybe a wet dream or two, but outside of that, I remember thinking 'damn.'

It was the one and only time I've ever been caught off guard with sex. So I guess by everyone's definition, that was the best sex I ever had, other than my wife."

The group all laughs as the attention turns to Chris, the only person who hadn't shared as of yet.

"Alright, big dog, fess up," Mitch says. "Give us your story."

Chris thinks for a moment and takes a sip of his beer. He's about to go into his story when Tracy walks out and interrupts the group looking for David.

"Hey, David, the firestick is acting up. Monica said you fixed it the last time it was acting funny," she says.

"Alright, I'll be there in a second. I wanna hear Chris's story first," he replies, piquing Tracy's interest.

"Chris's story? What are y'all up to out here?" A suspicious Tracy asks.

"Nothing much. We all were talking about the best sex we've ever had, outside of our wives, of course," Mitch explains. "We've all told our tales of glory, and we're waiting for our friend here to give his story."

An intrigued Tracy turns to Chris and looks on in anticipation of his story. Chris laughs as he looks around at the others.

"Oh, come on. We have a woman here," he says, trying to avoid going into a discussion with Tracy around.

"Trace is just like one of the fellas. Aren't you, Tracy?" Mitch responds, looking towards his partner.

"Yeah, I'm just one of the fellas. I'm just curious to hear a little guy talk," she quips as the group wait for Chris once again.

After a few moments, Chris sighs before going into his story.

"Fine. The best sex I ever had, other than my wife, was actually somebody I worked with," he admits, alluding to his days with Tracy.

Tracy freezes up, thinking Chris was about to go into their affair on live TV.

"It was the first job I ever had. Working at a retail store," Chris explains, relieving Tracy for the moment. "We were closing one night together, and it was her final day working there. She was moving out of town for school or something. I always felt we had a connection, but she had a boyfriend at the time, and I believe I was dating someone too."

"Oh, this is getting good," Mitch says, grinning. "Forbidden love."

"Yeah, well, I don't know about all that, but we got to talking about how we were going to miss each other, and all that. One thing lead to another, and we ended up having sex in the back of the warehouse floor," Chris tells the group, stunning them all.

"On the warehouse floor?" David asks as if he's disgusted by the act. "Do you know the amount of germs that are on a warehouse floor?"

"It didn't matter," Chris fires back. "All I could think about is this is the last time I'll ever see her, and I wanted to experience this with the little time I had with her."

The group can tell this was more than a run of the mill sexual encounter. It was real love and emotions behind Chris's tale.

"Sounds like she meant a lot to you," Gerald points out. "Did you ever try and track her down?"

"Nah. Like I said, we both had our relationships we were in," Chris reminds him. "If me and her would have met in different circumstances and all, who knows. Maybe my life would have been different. I mean, I can't complain because I have a wonderful wife right now, but sometimes fate is what it is. It's one of life's mysteries to wonder what could have happened. It wasn't just the sex we had that made it great. It was the emotion behind it, you know."

Tracy is struggling with her emotions as Chris's words about their secret relationship tore at her inside. For him to share that moment with the others, and not just her, meant a lot to her, hearing how much it all meant to him. Mitch looks at his partner and can tell she's getting a little weepy-eyed.

"Trace, you got a story you'd like to share with the fellas?" He said with a smirk.

"Huh? Um... no, I'm just... No, I'm good," Tracy replies, trying to keep her emotions in check.

"Come on, it's just us. It'll be nice to hear a woman's perspective," Mitch goads. "Tell us, what was the best sex you ever had, other than your husband."

Tracy is at a loss for words as she notices Chris is looking at her, wanting to hear what she had to say.

"Look, I'm not going to go into details. All I say is this, the best sex I ever had come from a guy I really cared about, and it didn't work out beyond that," she says before turning back to David. "Whenever you can, David. We need your assistance inside."

David sighs as he gets up and follows Tracy back into the house to assist the ladies. As soon as the door is closed, Mitch chuckles hearing Tracy's story.

"And that is why we don't have discussions like that with women," he says. "Sex is too emotional for them. Never a wham, bam, thank you ma'am story. Always a sad tale."

"Sometimes it can be hard," Chris responds before rising. "I'm gonna get me another. Anyone wants one?"

"I'll take one," Sebastian says.

Mitch and Gerald wave Chris off before he makes his way back into the house to grab him and Sebastian another beer. As he walks in, he peeks in the living room watching as the ladies are all talking amongst each other except for Tracy, who is sitting at the end of the couch deep in her thoughts. He can tell that his little story spoke to her, and had her wondering about a few things. After several moments, he walks off and heads to the kitchen to fill their drink orders.

Back in Dallas, Alexis is looking through her phone on social media with the TV playing in the background while watching her son play games on his iPad out the corner of her eye. As she scrolls through Facebook, her attention is grabbed when a Team Experiment commercial comes on, teasing the next episode. It reveals that two contestants have had a past affair with each other, which causes her to smile with intrigue. The teaser flashes all the contestants with a question mark, advising the audience to stay tuned for the shocking reveal.

"I bet it's Victoria and Mitch," Alexis mumbles to herself. "Them two look like they got something going on."

After a few moments, she shakes her head before scrolling on her phone once again, looking at the gossip sites trying to see if there is any information in reference to who the secret couple on the show is.

Margie is sitting in the main conference room of the WBC Studios office, sick to her stomach after watching the promo that just aired. She can't believe the show is allowing this humiliation, essentially ruining both Chris and Tracy's lives. After several moments, Dunbar makes his way into the conference room talking on his cell phone. The way he's sucking up to the caller leads Margie to believe that he's talking to Mr. Brooks. After several moments, Dunbar hangs up the phone with excitement.

"Did you see the spot?" He asks his assistant. "Can you imagine what this build-up is going to do for our ratings?"

"Sir, it's still not too late to back out," Margie points out. "We can still do the right thing by-"

"Noted," Dunbar interrupts before taking a seat across from her. "So, is everything set up for tomorrow?"

"Yes, the trivia competition is a go," Margie informs. "Chris and Tracy will interact once again, after which Melissa will interview Chris to see if he wants to make a team change."

"Which he will," Dunbar says with confidence. "And once he does, I want every strategy room meeting between the two sent to me directly. We're going to try and angle it as a tale of tortured love. If the two end up having sex, it would be even better!"

"Sir, this is still a family show," Margie reminds her boss. "You can't just have people having sex on network television."

"I'm not an idiot, Margie. It'll just be hinted they had sex," Dunbar replies. "Let the crew know if they have sex, I want to know about it as soon as it happens. Wake me up at two in the morning if they have to, but I want to know about it immediately."

Dunbar is feeling himself with a sinister smirk on his face.

"What if he doesn't, sir?" Margie asks her boss. "I mean, what if he decides to stay with Julia? Or pick someone else? This could all be for nothing if he does that."

"It's your job to make sure he does," Dunbar bellows.

"I can't make him pick anyone," Margie replies, much to the disdain of her boss. "If he knew what you were planning, he and Tracy could walk off the show."

"Margie, let me explain to you how this is going to work," Dunbar says as he walks over to her. "Tomorrow, Chris is going to make that selection. He's going to pick Tracy just as we want, and he's going to have conversations that will drive our ratings through the roof. If none of that happens by the end of the show, then I'll be instructing my new assistant on what I need to get done, because in case you've forgotten, my ass is on the line if this show fails. I'm willing to do whatever it takes for our plans to come together, and I suggest you start thinking the same."

Dunbar taps his assistant on the shoulder before making his way out of the office. Margie knows there's no way she can convince Chris to pick Tracy without ruining the reasons behind it. Her and Dunbar's fate was up to what Chris decides. Part of her hopes Chris doesn't select Tracy, but a small part of her hopes he would so she could keep her career going. The guilt begins to wear on Margie as she takes a deep breath and collects her things before making her way out of the conference room.

Chapter 8

The Decision

The next morning, Melissa is already in her chair getting her makeup together when Chris and a few others look on confused. Margie is giving directions to the crew when a curious Chris pulls her to the side.

"Hey, what's going on?" He questions.

"Oh, hey. Yeah, today's show is going to be taped instead of broadcast live," Margie explains. "We do that sometimes when we've double booked the crew."

"Oh. Well, thanks for telling us," Lucia, who is standing next to Chris, says.

"I'm sorry, I thought someone communicated that with you all," Margie replies as she looks around. "Look, we have about a half-hour before the shoot. Can you let the others know?"

"A half-hour? For five women to get ready? Are you serious?" Lucia responds as if she's offended. "You must be smokin', chica."

"Look, this is the hustle of live TV. Now you can spend

what little time you having arguing about it, or you can get prepared. It's up to you," Margie quips.

After a few moments, Lucia agrees and quickly makes her way off. Chris is about to walk off too when Margie grabs him by his arm and pulls him to the side.

"Hey, look, after today's event, you're going to sit down with Melissa and talk about if you're changing teammates or not," she explains to him. "Do you have a clue on what you're going to do?"

"I mean, I have a couple of ideas about what I'm going to do, but I'm still on the fence. I guess I'll see how things go after this competition," Chris replies, lying about his intentions.

"Okay, good. I hope you make the right call," she says. "A lot of money is at stake, but go with your heart, okay?"

Chris looks at Margie strangely, getting a vibe from her that he's not understanding. He slowly nods his head and walks off to prepare for the next event.

Thirty minutes later, the contestants are all in the back yard ready for their next competition. The men sit at a mock interrogation table across from the women, with Melissa, ready to start taping.

"Welcome back! Now, as discussed earlier, Chris has a decision to make following today's competition. Currently, he and Julia are in the lead with two hundred points, followed by Tracy and Mitch with seventy-five points. It's still anyone's game, as today the ladies are going to get their chance to earn points for their perspective teams," Melissa says before turning towards the ladies. "What you're going to play today is Three Questions. It's your job to find out the answers to your opponent's four key categories: Favorite Food, Favorite Sport, Childhood Hero, and finally Favorite Color. In your hand is a list of one hundred answers for each category. Each question is worth a total of one hundred points, but for each question you ask, you lose twenty-five winnable points for that category. So, for example, if you're able to get the correct answer by asking just one question, you'll be awarded seventy-five points for that category. Keep in mind, you only get one chance to guess, and men, you must answer the question truthfully. Also, just to mention it, the only question you can't ask is the main question itself."

The group all chuckle as Melissa continues with the presentation.

"Okay, ladies. We're going to give you a little revenge. You'll be paired against the same men that tickled you on the last event," she explains, causing Tracy to drop her head and Chris to smile. "Good luck, ladies. Monica, you're up first. Your opponent is Sebastian."

Monica steps forward and looks at her list trying to decide on the best question to ask her rival.

Thirty minutes have gone by with Tracy next in line to question Chris. So far, Monica has earned one hundred points for her team, Victoria has earned one hundred seventy-five points, and Lucia and Julia earned two hundred for their respective teams. Tracy looks across at Chris, who has a smirk on his face as Melissa approaches Tracy.

"Alright, Tracy, it's up to you. Currently, Lucia and Julia are in the lead in this event with two hundred points each. It's up to you to see if you can beat their mark," she presents as Tracy thinks for a moment.

"Melissa, do I really need to ask any questions?" Tracy asks. "I mean, is there a rule that I have to ask a question?"

"Technically, no. You don't have to ask anything, but remember you only get one chance to answer the questions correctly. If you're wrong, you forgo that category," Melissa responds.

"Fair enough," Tracy responds while tossing the list to the side. "I'm good at reading people, and I think I can read Chris real well."

"As you wish. Good luck," Melissa replies before allowing Tracy to question her victim.

"Let's start with the easiest question first," she says with a smirk. "Favorite sport is obviously football, am I correct?"

Chris nods his head with acknowledgment as Tracy continues.

"Now, favorite food is a little trickier. You look like you take care of yourself pretty well, but it's not above you to indulge every now and then. A lot of junk food would be canceled there because you are energetic for the most part, but something tells me you're a pizza man, right?" She asks.

"Two for two," Chris responds as Tracy nods her head with acknowledgment.

"Now favorite color. A typical guy's favorite color is blue, but you're different and pride yourself on it," she says, acting as though she's struggling. "You seem to like to set yourself apart from the norm, which would leave green, yellow, and orange. Orange is too much of a girl's color, so that's out. Money is green, but that's not your motivation in life. I'm going to go with yellow, right?"

"Perfect so far," Chris replies, which stuns Melissa and the rest of the contestants.

"Now favorite childhood character. That's the one I'm having the most difficulty with, especially since I'm not into the whole superhero thing. From the ones I do know, you're no Superman fan. You don't like to be the center of attention from what I've seen since you've been here. Could be wrong there, but I think I'm pretty spot on. You aren't afraid to take risks to get what you want. No fear. Based on that, I'm going to take a wild guess and say your favorite childhood here is Batman. How did I do?"

Chris drops his head and laughs as everyone anticipates his answer.

"Is she correct, Chris?" Melissa asks.

"One hundred percent," he replies with a smirk.

"Wow! I can't believe it. Four in a row, ladies and gentlemen!" Melissa exclaims as she pulls Tracy to the side. "Unbelievable! You just earned your team four hundred points, which allows you to keep the heat on Chris and Julia. Your team needed a boost and you sure got it! How were you able to pull off such a wonderful feat?"

"I just have a knack for reading people, that's all," Tracy responds with a smile.

"Well, remind me never to play poker with you," Melissa jokes before turning her attention back to the camera. "Seems like we have a two team battle for first place as team one has four hundred seventy-five points versus team five who are still holding a strong lead of six hundred points. Will he give up that lead to swap partners? Find out when we return!"

The camera operator yells clear as Tracy walks off and joins the rest of the contestants. Her and Mitch celebrate as everyone is stunned she was able to dominate the question competition as she did. Chris is about to join them when Melissa pulls him to this side.

"Okay, when we start taping again, you'll go ahead and announce your decision to the viewers. Please try and act like this is a hard choice to make," Melissa explains while her makeup artist tries to give her a brief touch up.

"What are you talking about? This is a hard decision." A

confused Chris responds.

"Not from what I heard," Melissa quips with a smirk.

A befuddled Chris looks on as the camera crew starts the countdown to start the taping once again. A crew member jerks Chris's arm and positions him in the camera frame and jumps out of the way just at the camera begins recording.

"Welcome back, everyone. I'm standing here with Chris, who has to finally decide whether he wants to keep his current teammate Julia, or swap her for either Monica, Lucia, Tracy, or Victoria," Melissa says before turning her attention with Chris. "Now, Chris, you've had time to meet with each of the contestants in the strategy room this week. Your team is currently in the lead with six hundred points, which means if you swap Julia from your team, you'll lose the lead. The question that everyone at home wants to know is are you willing to make a switch, and if so, who is joining your team?"

Everyone is silent as Chris acts as though he's struggling with his decision. Margie is in the Team Experiment house peering out of the window, hoping Chris doesn't take the bait. It's the one thing that might be able to sway Dunbar from running the promo he wants to. After several moments, Chris sighs as he turns to Melissa.

"I'm not going to lie, this is a tough decision," Chris says. "I mean, me and Julia have a good thing going, and I love her competitive spirit. All the ladies are full of fun and energy, and although this will leave me at a disadvantage temporarily, I'm going to use my power and swap partners to Tracy."

Margie backs away from the window disappointed with Chris as the other contestants mostly are shocked as well. The only two that aren't stunned by the decision are Tracy and Victoria. Julia is especially stunned, wondering why Chris would break up their team and sacrifice the lead they had on the others.

"Now, Chris, next week is the first elimination battle. Currently, as the leading team, you have the power to nominate two teams to battle each other where the losing team is sent home. By trading partners, you're giving that power to Julia and Mitch. Is that your final decision?" Melissa asks, giving Chris one last chance.

"Yes, I think it is," Chris says, acting as if he's uncertain.

"Okay. Well, Tracy is now officially your new partner," Melissa announces. "That means Julia and Mitch are officially partners now. Julia takes the six hundred points earned between you two to Mitch, and Tracy brings with her four hundred and seventy-five points."

Chris nods his head as Melissa turns to the camera.

"This is a stunning turn of events, ladies and gentlemen! Will the decision to swap to Tracy come back and bite him with the first elimination looming? Find out next week as the new team leaders Julia and Mitch nominate two teams to battle elimination," Melissa hypes up before wrapping up the taping.

After the cameras are clear, Melissa is about to hurry off when Chris runs up to her and pulls her off to the side.

"Hey, real quick, that comment you made before we went on air, what did you mean by that?" He asks.

"What comment?" Melissa asks.

"You know that *not from what I heard* comment you made when I told you this was going to be a difficult decision," Chris explains. "What was that about?"

"Look, I'm late to an appointment already, thanks to the show moving taping today. I don't have time for this or know what you're referring to. If you have any questions, get with

Margie. She's here for anything you need," Melissa quips before walking off, leaving Chris hanging.

Chris scratches his head with confusion before making his way into the house. He notices Tracy sitting at the bar area of the kitchen alone eating an apple with her head held low. He makes his way over, trying to not look suspicious, and takes a seat next to her.

"So, I guess we're partners now," he says with a smirk.

"I told you not to do that," Tracy remarks. "I don't see how stupid you can be. I mean, what if somebody puts things together that we-"

"Cameras, remember!" Chris says, cutting off his new teammate. "Look, why don't we take this to the strategy room and talk about how we're going to win this thing."

Tracy gives Chris an evil stare before tossing the apple core in a nearby garbage can and rising from her stool. Chris nods as he leads the way to the strategy room.

Once in the room, Tracy walks over and takes a seat on the couch with a hint of attitude as the two remain silent. After a few moments, Chris begins to chuckle to himself, confusing Tracy.

"What's so funny?" She asks.

"I know how to read people?" Chris mocks, referring to Tracy's earlier comments. "Why not just tell the world we fucked once? Seriously, what were you thinking?"

"Well, what about your ear thing?" Tracy fires back. "You don't think that drew suspicion? I couldn't for the life of me figure out how you knew about that, but then it dawned on me. That night we hooked up. You were stroking my hair and accidentally touched my ear."

"Yeah, you almost busted a gut laughing. Couldn't believe how serious it was until the competition," Chris smirks.

"My point is you were showing too much knowledge about me. I mean, even the slowest people are probably questioning us now," Tracy points out.

"And your 'I know how to read people' didn't show we know each other?" Chris replies. "I mean, come on, Trace."

"I only did that to get you back for the ear thing," Tracy admits. "Besides, I told you I didn't want you to pick me! I thought you got the picture when you were all snuggled up with your boo, Victoria!"

Chris looks at Tracy strangely before taking a seat next to her.

"What are you talking about?" He inquires.

"At the side of the pool the other night. I saw how you and her were all friendly. Figured you'd take her fast ass," Tracy says with a hint of jealousy. "Then you got the nerve to tell that bullshit story about the best sex you ever had besides your wife was with me? Trying to get me in my feelings. I can't believe I fell for you! Should have known you're no good just like the rest of these dudes out here."

"Whoa, whoa, back up a minute," Chris responds. "Look, I don't know what you think you saw, but I'm not into Victoria whatsoever."

"Didn't look like it that night," Tracy replies.

"Trace, Victoria is trying to make it as a reality star. She doesn't care about any of this," Chris reveals. "When me and her talked in here, she said she wants to win the money, but she's more interested in being popular. All that flirty shit she's doing is for the cameras."

Tracy isn't buying Chris's excuse choosing to sit with her arms folded, looking away from him. Chris shakes his head with disbelief before chuckling.

"Oh my god, you're jealous," he says with a smirk. "I can't believe it. You're actually sitting here jealous."

"I am not!" Tracy snaps back.

"Look at you. You're sitting with your arms folded, and won't even look me in my eyes," Chris points out.

Tracy slowly turns towards Chris and looks him in his eyes. After a few moments, she realizes that he's right, and she was jealous of what she saw that night. It didn't make sense to her since Chris wasn't her spouse. She slowly begins to come to terms with herself as Chris waits for a reaction.

"You're right. I'm sorry," she says. "I... I don't know where that is coming from."

"I know what it's coming from," Chris replies. "And I feel the same way. Tracy, look. I know what we did way back then wasn't the best decision we ever made, but there has to be something behind it. I mean, look at you. You were ready to bust my ass for having an interest in someone else. Not that I had one, mind you, but even you have to realize we've been given this second chance for a reason."

Tracy considers her old lover's words for a moment before shaking her head in denial.

"Chris, I told you not to pick me. I specifically told you that," she quips. "Why would you do this?"

"You know why," Chris says while scooting closer towards her. "It's the same reason you threw that first event. You're intrigued and want to see where this can go."

"And where do we go from here?" Tracy asks. "We're on

national television, Chris. It's not like we can live in this room. Not to mention we could be the ones going home next week. Either way, we're on borrowed time here."

"Then I suggest we enjoy the little time we have here before it's all gone," Chris replies as he puts his arms around his old friend.

Tracy hasn't felt this safe in someone's arms in a long time. With her and James on different pages in their marriage, feeling someone who genuinely cares for her felt foreign. She nestles into Chris feeling a vibe she hasn't felt since her final night at the cell phone shop.

"This is so wrong," she utters. "We're both married. This is so wrong on so many levels."

"We're not happy with our marriages," Chris admits. "You know it, and I know it. Like they say, you always go seeking what you're missing in a relationship from someone else. There are things we're missing in our marriage, and we seem to have found it with each other."

"So, what's missing in your marriage?" Tracy inquires.

Chris chuckles as Tracy lifts her head from his chest.

"You first," he replies.

Tracy sighs while thinking of her and James's relationship. She starts going into her story about feeling alone in her household, and how her husband doesn't show her any affection. She talks about having to carry the workload at times, feeling like she married a child. Chris nods his head with understanding as he goes into his underlying issue with his wife's inability to please him sexually. He speaks about when they first met she was spontaneous and fun. He noticed as the relationship grew, that spontaneous nature and sexual kink of hers started to disappear. He feels that he and she are in a rut, and she refuses to change her ways. Both Tracy and Chris feel a certain relief getting these issues off their chest feeling closer to each other than ever before.

Outside of the home, Melissa is setting up a taping, unknowingly to the house contestants as the cameraman cuts to her, letting her know she's being recorded.

"Hello, viewers! As we've been teasing all week, two of our contestants have known each other prior to the show. We didn't learn about it until after the show started, and we were stunned to learn about the history these two have hidden," Melissa says, building up tension.

The earlier taping is now showing on TV as Tracy's husband, James, is at the couple's apartment on the couch with the show running in the background as he's making out with another woman. The female removes her top and mounts James, much to his delight.

"Today we bring you a Team Experiment first as we tap into the secret Strategy Room Chronicles between these two former love birds. Check it out," Melissa says before the screen cuts to Chris and Tracy's first conversation in the strategy room.

James is into the female he's with until he hears his wife's voice on TV. He looks over and listens to the conversation. He's blown away hearing about the secret affair his wife had with Chris as anger and confusion fills his face. He pushes the female that was working him to the side, giving his full attention to the TV.

"What the fuck?!" He exclaims, becoming more upset by the moment.

Back in Dallas, in Chris's home, Alexis is in tears watching the same video feed that James is watching. She can't believe what she is hearing and is embarrassed with every passing moment. Her cell phone begins to ring, with family and friends trying to contact her to see if she is watching the events unfolding on TV. She ignores the calls and texts, stewing with anger as tears continue to fill her face, hearing about her husband's past infidelities.

Chapter 9

Elimination Day

Elimination day has approached as all the teams are lined up outside waiting for the broadcast to begin. Julia and Mitch are standing with Melissa as the countdown to go live begins. Over the past few days, Tracy and Chris have tried to keep a low profile, meeting on occasion just to keep up appearances. Both have tried to fight their feelings for one another, but the more time they spent together, the harder it's become. As the broadcast begins, Melissa turns her attention towards the leading team of Julia and Mitch.

"Okay, Julia and Mitch, you ended last week with the lead, and have earned the right to choose two teams who will battle for elimination," Melissa announces with a smile. "You've had time to process and think about it, so now America wants to know who are you selecting for the elimination round?"

"Well we thought about it, and we've decided we're putting up Tracy and Chris to battle Monica and Gerald," Julia responds with a smile.

Chris is confused after hearing the announcement looking towards Tracy who doesn't seem too concerned about it.

Melissa turns to the rest of the contestants with a smile.

"David, Lucia, Sebastian, and Victoria, you all can be seated as you are safe this go round," she says.

The contestants she called out all back away and take a seat at the lounging area leaving the two battling teams standing. Melissa turns her attention to the camera to continue to broadcast.

"These two teams will go head to head, where the loser will be sent packing. Will Chris and Tracy go home today, or will it be the team of Monica and Gerald who are sent home? Find out when we return!"

The cameraman yells clear as the production crew scrambles to set up the next event. A suspicious Chris pulls Tracy to the side.

"It doesn't make sense," he said.

"What?"

"I understand them putting us on the block since we're their biggest competition, but this whole Monica and Gerald thing doesn't make sense," he says while looking over at the lounging area.

He notices the non-competing team's interaction with each other when something clicks to him.

"Holy shit. The other teams have an alliance with each other," Chris points out.

"Alliance? I'm not understanding," Tracy replies.

"They made a pact with each other to throw us under the knife while they remain safe," Chris explains. "Like calling a truce to get others not in their little secret society chosen for elimination. It's all part of the show. I've been so concerned with other stuff that I haven't been actually playing the game."

Tracy nods her head, understanding what her partner was trying to explain to her. She looks over at the group and notices that Victoria and Mitch seem to be close as she whispers something in her ear, causing him to laugh.

"Mitch and Victoria seem to be real buddy-buddy right now," she says after her observation. "Seems like she's the reason they're off the block."

"Well, doesn't matter now. We need to focus to make sure we win this thing. I'm not ready to leave yet," Chris responds as he looks into Tracy's eyes. "I mean, there's so much more I want to... I really wanted a shot at that money."

Tracy understood her partner's concern wasn't the money. It was to spend more time together with each other. She nods her head as well, letting him know she understands.

"Yeah, me too," she said with a smirk. "But, maybe it's not our fate to win."

Chris chuckles at Tracy's use of the fate line.

"You don't believe that, and neither do I," he replies as they dap each other off.

The production motions the competing teams to a portion of the back yard with a nice view of the valley as the cameras are set up and ready to film. As Tracy and Chris walk to their assigned spots, Gerald approaches both of them with a smile.

"Well, it seems like one of us will be going home today," he says before shaking both of their hands. "I just want to say good luck to both of you."

"Yeah, you too," Chris responds.

Monica remains silent as she's not interested in wishing her opponents good luck. She's focused waiting for the competition to begin. She has tried for years to become a contestant on the show and wasn't interested in being sent home. Melissa walks over and gets ready for the camera as the countdown to return to the broadcast begins.

"Ok, we're back for our first elimination competition. Today's elimination battle will evolve around trivia. Chris and Tracy, since you have the higher score, you get to select the category in which to battle. Your choices are sports, geography, music, technology, and automotive. What's your choice going to be?"

Tracy and Chris have a quick huddle, coming to an agreement on the category selection.

"Melissa, we're going to go with music," Chris announces.

"Okay, music it is," Melissa repeats. "Since Tracy and Chris picked the category, Gerald and Monica will get the first chance to answer. How this works is there are one hundred possible questions that can be asked. You have to select a number between one and a hundred, and I'll read the question associated with that number. You will get a chance to answer a minimum of three questions each. The first team to get to three correct questions wins the competition. If there is a tie, we go to sudden death. The loser of the event is sent home, and out of the competition. Are there any questions?"

The competing teams shake their heads as Melissa pulls a sheet of questions labeled by number, just as she explained.

"Okay, Gerald and Monica, you're up. What number are you selecting?" She asks.

"Give us number fifty-nine," Monica replies.

"Okay. The question is, the illustrious music great Wolfgang Mozart was born on what date?" Melissa asks, stunning both Monica and Gerald.

Neither of them has a clue. Tracy and Chris also look

concerned, not expecting the level of questioning that was just asked. Gerald, not knowing what to respond, just blurts out the first date that comes to mind.

"May 13th?" He says.

"No, I'm sorry. The correct answer is January 27th, 1756." Melissa replies before turning to Chris and Tracy. "Chris and Tracy, you're up. Pick a number between one and a hundred, please."

"Give us sixteen, Melissa," Tracy replies.

"Okay, your question is this rapper turned actor was born on June 16th, 1971 and gunned down in Las Vegas in 1996 after attending a Mike Tyson fight. Who is this infamous entertainer?"

Chris and Tracy breathe a sigh of relief after hearing their question. Gerald and Monica are stunned with the ease of question their competitors got.

"That would be Tupac Shakur," Chris confidently answers.

"That is correct! You two have taken the early lead," Melissa replies before turning back to Monica and Gerald. "Monica, Gerald, please pick a number."

"Um, give us twelve I guess," Monica responds, hoping for good luck.

"Okay, your question is, what was the nickname of the great music composer Antonio Vivaldi?" Melissa asks, confusing Gerald and Monica once again.

"Who?" Gerald asks while scratching his head.

"Antonio Vivaldi," Melissa repeats.

Gerald looks towards Monica, who is just as clueless as he

is.

"Would that be Tony?" Monica answers, taking a shot in the dark.

"I'm sorry, that is incorrect. The correct answer is Il Prete Rosso or the Red Priest," Melissa responds.

Gerald and Monica look at each other in disbelief as Melissa turns her attention back to Tracy and Chris.

"Okay you two, what number will it be?" she asks.

"Give me lucky number seven," Chris says.

"Very well. Your question is, This Louisiana native started out her career as a Mouseketeer on the Disney channel, and is best known for such hits as 'Opps I did it Again', 'Baby One More Time', and 'Gimme More'. Who is this superstar?" Melissa asks, stunning Gerald and Monica once more.

"Melissa, would that be Brittany Spears?" Chris responds with confidence.

"That answer is correct! You now have a two point lead," Melissa responds as Tracy and Chris dap each other off.

Melissa turns her attention back towards Monica and Gerald, who both suspect something is up at this point.

"Gerald and Monica, please select your next number," she says.

"What the hell, give me number ten," Gerald says, disgusted with what's going on.

"Okay; this Destiny's Child singer not only has a number one single to her name but has acted on several sitcoms in her career. Who is this singer?"

Monica smiles, relieved to have been given an easy question.

"I know this one. That would be Beyonce Knowles," she says with confidence.

"I'm sorry, that is incorrect," Melissa responds, stunning Monica. "The correct answer is Kelly Rowland. The question stated she had a number one single. Beyonce has had multiple, and Kelly also had a recurring role on the sitcom 'The Hughleys', where Beyonce hasn't been on any sitcoms."

Gerald and Monica can't believe what they're hearing as Melissa turns her attention towards Chris and Tracy once more.

"Chris, Tracy, with one more correct answer, you can win the event and send Monica and Gerald home packing. What number are you selecting this time?"

"Give me number one," Chris says before taking a deep breath.

"Okay. The question is as follows; This once Bronx native was working in a strip club prior to breaking out on the hit show 'Love and Hip Hop: New York' as a rapper. Who is she?"

Tracy gets excited, knowing the answer to save them from elimination.

"Melissa, that would be Cardi B!" She exclaims, showing the first signs of excitement since joining the show.

"That is correct! And with that answer, you and Chris have just won the first elimination round, and are safe!"

Tracy pumps her first as she and Chris share a brief hug together in celebration. They tone down their celebration eventually, realizing that the cameras are still rolling. Melissa walks over to Gerald and Monica, who are both upset over the outcome.

"Gerald and Monica, unfortunately, your time with us is up," she says to the defeated team. "Please head in, and collect your things."

Melissa turns her attention to the camera once more with a smile.

"Coming up, we say our goodbyes to Monica and Gerald," she says.

The camera crew cuts the feed as Chris walks over to offer his condolences to the losing team.

"Hey, guys. Sorry to see you go," he says to them.

"I don't know what you guys have done, but it doesn't take a genius to see that game was fixed," Monica blasts back, rejecting Chris's words.

"Fixed? What are you talking about?" Tracy inquires as she steps forward.

"Don't play dumb with me! You're all in on it!" Monica fires back before huffing and puffing her way back towards the house.

The two are approached by Gerald, who shakes both of their hands before walking off himself. Chris and Tracy are confused about where the accusations are coming from as Victoria watches them from the distance, seeing Monica's blow up.

"Did you see that out there?" She whispers to her partner Sebastian.

"What?" He asks.

"That little blow up with Monica, Tracy, and Chris," she points out. "She seems pissed, and I know why. That last competition looked rigged. Something's not right with that."

"Yeah, I think it was just the luck of the draw," Sebastian responds, waving off any notion of wrongdoing. "Why would the show wanna throw the competition? It doesn't make sense."

"Baby, I've been trying to become a reality star for a minute now. One thing I will tell you reality isn't real," Victoria responds. "They want those two to remain on the show for some reason. I don't know why, but I think it's time we team up with them."

"Form an alliance with Tracy and Chris?" Sebastian inquires, looking around to make sure no one can hear them. "But we already have one with Mitch and Julia. Why would we mess that up?"

"I'm not saying we break our truce. What I'm saying is we form one with Tracy and Chris, and keep the one with Mitch and Julia. If I'm wrong, then we stand with our first deal. If I'm not, we can turn on Julia and Mitch when they least suspect it," a cryptic Julia explains. "Either way, we come out on top. What do you say?"

Sebastian thinks for a moment as his partner has a point. It would be a low-risk maneuver that could extend their stay, allowing them to have a chance at the prize money. After careful consideration, he nods his head with approval, much to Victoria's delight.

"So, how are we gonna approach them?" He asks.

"Leave that to me," Victoria responds with a smirk. "I'll get them on our side."

"Be careful," Sebastian warns. "If Julia and Mitch find out, it could backfire on us."

"Don't worry about that. I have game, baby. Nobody will know a thing," Victoria responds before getting up and walking off into the house.

Later that night, in Dunbar's office, he's checking his emails for the day, and many of them are enjoying his affair angle he's shown the world. The show's ratings have sky-rocketed after the reveal, and other private conversations between the two have been broadcast. An exhausted Margie knocks on the door before making her way in. She plops down in the seat across from her boss struggling to keep her eyes open.

"Boss, you wanted to see me?" She asks.

"Yes! Good news! The show is a success!" Dunbar exclaims. "They just love Chris and Tracy! The response has been nothing but positive, with the exception of one person."

"Who?" Margie asks mid-yawn.

"Chris's wife, Alexis," Dunbar reveals. "She's been pitching a fit all week, upset on what's going on."

"Well, can't say I'm surprised by it," Margie says with an 'I told you so' attitude. "So what are you going to do about it?"

"Not what am I going to do. It's what you're going to do," Dunbar quips, surprising Margie. "She's been calling the office every day since the reveal. She's finally come out this way and is staying at the Sheraton by LAX. I told her you will be available to meet with her tomorrow morning."

"Tomorrow morning?!" Margie fires back, stunned at the news. "Sir, do you realize what time I would have to wake up to beat the traffic to get here at eight? Not to mention I have to drive way back to the house to overlook the show afterward?"

"Those are the breaks, Margie," Dunbar replies, not caring about his assistant's concern. "It shouldn't take you long. We have Chris's signed paperwork absolving us from everything. You can bring her a copy to review by her lawyer if she wants. Offer to pay for her hotel stay and a free tour of the studio lot."

"You're exploiting her husband's affair and embarrassing her to the entire world, and your thought is to offer her a guided tour?" Margie replies in amazement.

"Whatever it takes," Dunbar responds. "We've already surpassed last season's top-ranking, which was the season's finale. Can you imagine the ratings when these two are in the finals?"

"That's another thing. I can't keep fixing these events," Margie quips. "I mean, it was so obvious what we're doing. How long do you think it'll take before the other contestants catch on?"

"Don't know, and don't care," a nonchalant Dunbar responds. "Get them to the finals. After that, I don't care who wins. If they do, great! If they don't, oh well. Either way, the ratings are going to be through the roof."

Margie is about to respond when she realizes nothing she can say would change her boss's mood. After a few moments, she slowly rises and starts to make her way out of the office. Dunbar goes back to checking his email and giggling like a schoolgirl reading the amazing feedback he's getting.

Later that night, Tracy is asleep in her bed with a slight smirk on her face. She's dreaming about being in the strategy room with Chris, who has taken control of her, kissing her while pinning her to the wall. After a few moments of passionately kissing her, he leads her over to the couch and gently lies her down before aggressively ripping open her dress. The smirk grows as she envisions him taking off his pants and underwear and inserting himself inside her. Tracy's hand slowly begins to make it down to her midsection as the dream has her excited. She sees Chris grinding on her taking over every part of their interaction, leaving her helpless and a slave to his touch. Just as Tracy is about to have an orgasm, it's stolen from her as the dream ends, waking her up. She looks around the room and notices all the other ladies were in their beds asleep before realizing everything she saw was a dream.

After a few moments of thinking about the sexual vision she had, she sits up in bed and puts on her slippers before making it out of the room. Victoria, who was across from her, is awakened by the door opening and notices Tracy has left her bed. She quickly jumps out of bed and follows her.

In the kitchen, Tracy is getting her some water when she's startled by Victoria, who silently snuck up on her.

"Oh shit!" Tracy exclaimed. "You scared the shit out of me!"

"My bad, sorry, "Victoria says, trying to keep Tracy quiet. "I saw you were up and wanted to see if I could get with you about something."

Tracy nods her head as Victoria is about to take a seat on a nearby barstool before an idea hits her.

"Let's take a walk," she says, motioning Tracy to join her in the back yard.

Tracy looks at her suspiciously but follows her nonetheless as they make their way out of the house. There's a slight breeze in the air that sends chills down Tracy's back as Victoria leads her to the side of the house where there is a small corner spot where the house and fence connect. Victoria makes her way in the corner and motions Tracy to join her.

"My god, it's freezing out here," Tracy responds, clutching herself, trying to remain warm.

"I know, this SoCal weather is crazy," Victoria says with a smile. "I found this spot out when researching. This is the only spot on the premises where a camera or mic isn't placed, according to former cast and crew members. All kinds of shit happened here from what I read. It's a blind spot, so we can talk about a few things without anyone knowing. Me and Mitch have been here a couple of times having friendly conversations if you know what I mean."

"Okay?" A confused Tracy responds disgusted by Victoria's revelation. "So why am I here?"

"Me and Sebastian wanna join you and Chris in an alliance," Victoria reveals. "Wanted to see if you were interested."

"Oh, you mean an alliance like you have with Mitch and Julia," Tracy quips.

"We were that obvious?" Victoria responds with a smirk.

"Pretty much. Now that you've mentioned your little meetings with him, it makes even more sense," Tracy fires back, causing Victoria to laugh.

"By any means necessary," a sly Victoria replies.

Tracy nods her head as she ponders the proposition.

"I'll get with Chris and see what he thinks," she said.

"Alright, well, just give me the nod either way and let us know. It could be us in the finals. After that, all bets are off," Victoria replies as she shakes Tracy's hand.

She's about to walk off when Tracy pulls her back into the secluded corner.

"Hey, this is going to sound crazy, but… I don't know, I guess you might be the only person in this house who understands," Tracy says with a look of conflict in her eyes. "I can't believe I'm asking this, but how do you feel when you're doing your thing, like with Mitch?"

"My thing?" A perplexed Victoria asks.

"Yeah, you know. You and Mitch's friendly meetings, or whatever you called it? It doesn't make you feel guilty or anything?" Tracy struggles to ask, piquing Victoria's interest.

"Oh, my god. You're talking about Chris, aren't you?" she deduces.

"No, that's not what I'm talking about. I was just-"

"Bullshit! I could tell y'all had something going on," Victoria replies with a smirk. "You're into him, aren't you? That's why you're asking about feeling guilty."

"This... this was a mistake, I'm sorry," Tracy responds with embarrassment.

She's about to walk off when Victoria stops her.

"Hey. Chill out a minute," she says as Tracy calms down a bit.

"Look, I know you and the other girls think I'm out here hoeing, and doing all the nasty with the fellas," Victoria says as she leans on the house. "I get it, I really do. I know how it looks in your eyes. The fact that you're asking me this says you're feeling some type of way. Not about me, but how can I do what I do and not feel guilty. Well, check this out, I bet you got a husband on the outside that doesn't pay you any attention, doesn't fuck you at all, and just drags you down emotionally every day. Am I close?"

Tracy's face says it all. It's like Victoria has inside information on her life. What she described is exactly what Tracy was going through. Victoria smiles, taking Tracy's silence as confirmation.

"Like I said, I get it. It's crazy. You give them everything you have in life, and they still treat you like shit," Victoria replies, describing her own experience. "At a certain point in time, you have to do you. My husband was my life until he wasn't. I did everything to support him, and guess what he did? He fucked a friend of mine, talking about it was an accident. Like how do you accidentally fuck another person?"

Victoria shakes her head in disbelief, still hurting over her husband's infidelities. After taking a few moments to gather herself, she forces a smile on her face trying to hide the pain in her eyes.

"I know it's crazy, but me doing what I'm doing helps me forget my situation," she admits. "Having a guy all into you just means the world to me. I know it's all about sex with men, but I do what I have to do just to get a little feeling of worth. So, to answer your question about guilt, he didn't feel guilty doing what he did treating me like I'm worthless, so I don't feel guilty about doing me."

Tracy feels bad judging Victoria for her actions in the house. She can relate to feeling worthlessness in her relationship. Still, Tracy is curious about one aspect of Victoria's infidelities.

"What about Mitch?" She asks. "I mean, he's married too. You don't feel guilty about his family?"

Victoria chuckles and sighs.

"My dear Tracy," she says with glee. "It's not a one-way thing. He chose this path, not me. I didn't force him to do anything he didn't want to do. Why should I feel guilty about his family when he doesn't feel guilty about it?"

Tracy slowly nods her head even though she doesn't fully agree. Initially, in the back of her mind, Chris's family still matters to her. The more she thinks about it, however, the more Victoria makes sense. Why should she care about Chris's family? He's the one pushing the whole 'fate' idea. Tracy was willing to walk away from the show, but he convinced her otherwise. A slight breeze flows through the yard once again, causing Tracy to shiver.

"Shit, let me get back in this house," Tracy says. "I really appreciate you answering my question. I know that must have been difficult. I guess you really can't judge a book by its cover."

"Not when you're on the outside looking in," Victoria replies with a wink.

Tracy chuckles as she and Victoria quickly make their way back into the home. Victoria's words opened up Tracy's mind about her situation, and she knew she has two options. Either embrace Chris with her heart going where he wants to go with their relationship, or let him go forever, and possibly live with regret for the rest of her days.

Chapter 10

Opposite Ends

An infuriated Alexis is sitting in the WBC Building Lobby waiting to be seen by one of the network executives. She's stewing over the fact that she's been made to look like a fool in the eyes of everyone due to the exploits of the network and was there to get her husband pulled from the show. She checks the time on her phone, impatient after already sitting for an hour. Margie walks in looking unprepared after sitting in traffic trying to make it to the office on time when she notices Alexis sitting in the waiting area, and quickly approaches her.

"Hello, Ms. Sargent, I presume?" She says, extending her hand.

Alexis looks at Margie with a scowl on her face, uninterested in sharing pleasantries.

"I've been sitting here for an hour," she quips.

"I do apologize. I'm not sure if you've ever been to L.A. before, but the traffic can get a little hectic, especially in the-"

"Look, I'm not here for that shit! I want my husband pulled from the show, right fucking now!" Alexis exclaims, causing Margie to look around the area.

"Let's take this in the office, shall we?" Margie requests, looking to limit any distractions that may come from their discussion.

Alexis thinks for a moment before following Margie into the office, and into a nearby conference room. Marge takes a seat at the head of the table, a position she normally never has, as Alexis takes a seat adjacent to her, with her face still filled with anger.

"So, can I get you anything? A water or coffee?" Margie offers.

"Yeah, you can get me my husband off your show," Alexis fires back, rejecting Margie's pleasantries. "I can't believe you people would do this!"

"Ms. Sargent, I know you're upset, and I get it," Margie responds, trying to calm the furious wife.

"Do you?" Alexis quips. "Do you know how it feels to be embarrassed on national TV? In front of all your friends and family? Can you really understand how that feels? My life is in shambles right now! And for what? So you can boost your ratings? Do you even care what you people are doing to me and my husband?"

"Ms. Sargent, I understand how you feel," an emphatic Margie replies. "The thing is, your husband signed the waivers agreeing to it. Legally the show is within our rights to broadcast anything filmed on the property."

Alexis slams her fist on the table in frustration, frightening Margie who slid her chair slowly away from the angered wife.

"He didn't sign up for this shit and you know it!" Alexis exclaims. "I don't know how you dug up this dirt on him and that whore, but I want him off the show right now!"

"Unfortunately, right now, that's not plausible," a cautious Margie responds, hoping to avoid Alexis's wrath. "I mean, with the competitions and everything, he may be home early anyway. We're very clear when signing the paperwork that we can use the footage as we see fit, and no storyline is off the table. For the record, we didn't know anything about Chris and Tracy's previous... well, them knowing each other until they were already on the show. We didn't plan for this. I know it's hard and everything, but we have full documentation to back us."

Alexis jumps out of her chair and slowly approaches Margie sending chills down her spine. She seems to want to attack the executive as Margie braces for the assault. After a few threatening moments, a few tears start to slowly roll down Alexis's face as she backs away.

"Fine, you want to do it that way. You'll be hearing from my attorney," she says before storming out of the conference room.

Margie breathes a sigh of relief as she leans back in her chair trying to gather her thoughts. Although she is playing hardball for the network, she wholeheartedly agreed with Alexis. After a few moments of gathering herself, she takes out her cell phone and dials Dunbar, with a hint of disgust.

"It's done," she says before abruptly hanging up the phone.

She checks the time before finally rising and making her way out of the office and towards the Team Experiment House.

Later that evening, Tracy and Chris have their scheduled time in the strategy room as Tracy's thoughts begin to betray her morals. Victoria's discussion with her is still in the back of her mind, and she didn't know what she should do with Chris going forward. She initially decides against pursuing her feelings, but once she has seen him alone for the first time all to herself, she can no longer hold back. As soon as they make it into the room, an aggressive Tracy attacks Chris with a passionate kiss, catching him off guard. After a few moments of going back and forth, a stunned Chris finally backs away with a smirk.

"Well, damn," he says still trying to gather what just happened. "Can't say I expected that. Where did that come from?"

"I... I don't know what came over me," Tracy responds, embarrassed. "I... I've just been thinking about you a lot lately, and I know you said stuff about fate and everything... it's just... I don't know, I shouldn't have done that."

Tracy is about to walk off when Chris pulls her back.

"Hey, don't apologize for anything," Chris replies. "I'd be lying if I said I wasn't thinking about you. I just figured after we last talked that you weren't interested in rekindling those old feelings."

"I'm not. Well, I mean, I wasn't, but... I don't know, maybe I am," a confused Tracy says before taking a seat on the familiar couch.

Chris sits next to her, knowing she's struggling with her feelings.

"What changed?" He asks. "I mean, before I had to beg you to stay, and now you're greeting me with kisses? You can see why I'm a little confused here."

Tracy lowers her head, ashamed at giving in to her feelings for her longtime friend.

"I know, my bad. I didn't mean to," an apologetic Tracy responds. "I'm not trying to confuse you or anything. I really wish I could be selfish here, but even sitting here now battling these feelings for you, I look in your eyes, and all I see is your wife and child."

"Didn't stop you back at the cell shop," Chris points out.

"Yeah, that was different," Tracy retorts. "I didn't think I would see you again, so I didn't have to look in your eyes daily."

A smirking Chris slowly moves in and kisses Tracy once more, this time catching her off guard. Tracy doesn't fight it, enjoying the intimate moment. After a few seconds, Chris backs away from her and looks deep into her eyes.

"What do you see now?" He asks a conflicted Tracy.

"Please, Chris. Please don't make me do this," she pleas to him. "At this moment right now, I wouldn't fight it, and as much as my body wants it, I don't think my soul can survive it."

Chris thinks for a moment, knowing that his once lover is vulnerable right now. He would love nothing more than to take her on the couch at that very moment. She is practically inviting him in. After several moments, however, he didn't want to push it on her. He could tell the guilt she is already carrying and didn't want to be the one that makes her break that moral code she has.

"Damn, you know how to make things hard, don't you?" Chris says, pointing down to his crouch. "Literally, you know how to make things hard."

Tracy giggles as the sexual tension between the two starts to fade. Chris takes a deep breath as he checks the time on a nearby clock.

"So, is this how it's gonna be for us?" Chris asks. "Are we go back and forth with this as long as we're here?"

"We could always leave the show like I suggested," Tracy responds with a smirk. "I mean then, maybe I wouldn't feel as guilty if we did hook up."

"So you're basically telling me, if you knew we only had one night left together, you would get down with me without all the moral mumbo jumbo you're feeling now?" Chris asks, causing Tracy to laugh.

"It's not mumbo jumbo," she quips. "Besides, you could have had me just a second ago. Seems to me you're conflicted with this just like me."

"Well, you're not wrong," Chris admits as he gets comfortable. "I thought about a lot of things that you said, and I was coming here to tell you I wouldn't pressure you anymore. That was, however, before I was attacked."

"Wow, this is awkward," Tracy replies. "Here I am, ready to let loose on you, and here you were about to tell me that you were going to lay back. What's wrong with this picture?"

Chris chuckles at the ironic twist of fate.

"Damn, didn't think about it that way," he said, smirking.

Tracy sighs as she thinks for a moment. Even though she's happy that Chris is backing away sparing them the awkwardness of their sexual tension, she still can't help thinking about him. Victoria's words swirl in her head, as an idea suddenly pops in her head.

"Maybe there's a way we both can have what we want," she says, piquing her teammate's interest. "What if we wait until our final day on the show? I mean the exact day before we're to leave. By that time, we'll know it'll be our final moments together, and we can get together knowing it'll be the last time we see each other. We can hook up with each other one last time without all the awkwardness of having to see each other afterward if that makes sense."

Chris remains silent as he processes Tracy's offer. It'll give him one last shot with her, which is what he wanted. Also, not making things difficult on her which is his main concern. The plan is almost full proof, with one flaw.

"The problem I see is that we may not know when our last day will be," Chris points out. "I mean, we could be eliminated at any time on the show. If we are, we won't have the chance to hook up."

Tracy smiles as she surprises Chris by quickly mounting him on the couch. She leans in and kisses him on his neck, a spot that she knows he's vulnerable to. After several seductive kisses, she makes her way to his ear.

"Then it's not fate," she whispers to him.

Chris, still surprised by his partner's aggressiveness slowly nods his head with agreement. Tracy dismounts him and takes her seat next to him once again.

"What if we wait, and you decide to change your mind?" Chris inquires. "I mean, let's face it, you have been back and forth with this just in this conversation alone. What if we do have a chance, and you decide to back out?"

"What if you decide to back out?" Tracy fires back. "You're the one with a kid, Chris. My marriage is a joke, but you, you're the one who has to live with it."

"Yeah, I get that, but I've been living with it for the last two years," Chris points out.

"That's because it was a heat of the moment thing. This is planned out. It's going to give you a lot to think about between now and then. Thoughts change. People change. I'm not saying I won't change my mind too, but I'm just putting that out there for you to consider as well."

The two lovers are silent as thoughts begin racing in both of their heads. Chris sighs, as he decides on a proposal of his own.

"Tell you what, since we're going to only do this when we know it's our last day in the house, let's just make a decision when it gets here," Chris suggests. "I mean, if it is fate, and we do have that option, we can decide then on it. Right now, I think we need to keep our heads in the game and try and win this thing. Without that, nothing else matters, don't you think?"

Tracy nods her head with agreement.

"I guess it makes sense," she says. "On that note, Victoria and Sebastian want to join us in an alliance. She pitched it to me last night. Told her I'd get with you."

"I thought they already had their alliance," Chris responds, getting his head back into the game.

"They do, but they seem to think they'd fare better with us," Tracy answers. "I mean, if they can help us take care of Julia and Mitch, I think it'd be worth a shot. I'm not too concerned about Lucia and David, but Julia and Mitch, getting rid of them would definitely help us win this thing."

"It could backfire," Chris warns. "They may be playing us."

"I don't think they are. Call me crazy, but I believe Victoria's intentions," Tracy says.

Chris ponders for a few moments before finally nodding to his partner.

"Alright, I'm down. Look at us. Finally using the strategy room for its intended purpose," he jokes. "So, we're on the same page now. Game and otherwise?"

"Yeah, I guess we are," Tracy says with a smile.

She's about to rise from the couch when Chris pulls her back down. He pulls her on top of him once again, trying to regain their earlier magic.

"So, any chance of a little make-out session before we

bounce?" he says with a cryptic smile. "Nothing serious, just some of that old school high school make-out sessions."

"I lost my virginity at fourteen," Tracy replies, shocking Chris. "My high school sessions were serious."

Tracy dismounts Chris once more and rises from the couch.

"You want anything from me, then you go out there and play this game," she says, looking down at her lover, noticing the bulge coming from his shorts. "Business first, and then maybe I'll take care of your friend down there."

She winks before making her way out of the strategy room, leaving Chris frustrated and erect.

Tracy makes her way into the kitchen bar area where Victoria and Julia are sitting watching Lucia cook dinner for the household. She takes a seat next to Julia, who has a sinister grin on her face.

"I see you're returning from the strategy room," she says. "You two seem to use that room an awful lot. Is there anything you'd like to share with us?"

"Anything like what?" Tracy asks.

"I don't know. He's a handsome man; you're a cute girl. I don't blame you, of course, for spending time with him. He is chiseled in all the right places," Julia says as she notices Chris walking out of the strategy room and into the living room where the other male contestants were. "I'm actually jealous. I only had him the once in the strategy room. I guess I'm not his type though."

"Stop it, girl. They're just playing the game, that's all," Victoria says, defending Tracy. "They just wanna win like the rest of us."

"Maybe, but let's be honest here, me and Chris had the advantage. He gave up the lead just to be with her, which means maybe there's a little something there," a sinister Julia rebuts. "Come on, girlie. Fess up. What's up with you two?"

"Yeah, Mamacita. Give us the tea," Lucia chimes in. "We wanna know about Mr. Chocolate."

Tracy sighs and shakes her head in denial.

"There isn't anything going on between me and Chris," she replies. "And even if there was something going on, what makes you think I'd tell you all with the entire house wired? Come on now."

"Oh, I get it. You can't say 'cause of the camera. I got you, boo," Lucia says with a wink.

"Seriously, there isn't anything going on. I promise you," Tracy says.

"If you say so," an unconvinced Julia says. "If they have a switch mode again for the women, I promise you I'll switch with you with a quickness."

"Why? You and Mitch have been kicking ass. Why would you want to switch?" Tracy inquires.

"Because sometimes coffee needs a little cream," Julia answers, smirking. "Not that I would act on it, mind you, but I wouldn't mind the eye candy while I'm here."

"And Mitch isn't eye candy?" Tracy points out.

Right on cue, Mitch walks over and greets everyone before walking over to Victoria and whispering something in her ear. She starts to giggle as he makes his way outside of the home. After a few moments, Victoria quietly gets up and makes her way outside of the home as well, heading for the dead zone spot to meet with Mitch. Lucia rolls her eyes as she continues working on the meal prep.

"Well, someone definitely believes he's eye candy," she says, causing Julia to laugh. "I'm just saying, it's pretty obvious at this point, wouldn't you agree?"

"Hey, ease up on her. We don't know what she's been through," Tracy says. "We don't even know if it's that. Maybe she's just found someone in this house that she connects with. People always believe the worst of a situation."

"Yeah, I bet she is connecting with him," Lucia says with a giggle.

Tracy shakes her head as Julia notices her mood.

"You and Vikki seem to be real friendly lately," a suspicious Julia points out. "Care to comment on that?"

"All I'm saying is you don't know what people are going through. In this house, we're locked in, so to speak. It can feel like jail for some of us. For others, this is the freest they've ever been. They may want to have all the fun they can before the dream ends," Tracy explains, referring to not only Victoria but herself as well.

"Yeah, we'll see how much fun mami has when her husband finds out what she's been doing," Lucia responds. "To talk about men is one thing. To do whatever it is she's doing is another."

Tracy rolls her eyes as she gets up from the stool and heads back to the female room. Julia and Lucia share a look, nodding their heads.

"They've teamed up," Julia whispers, trying not to draw attention. "One minute she's hating on Victoria, the next minute she's defending her. I mean, what else could it be?"

"Maybe since Victoria isn't after her man anymore, she's fine with her," Lucia responds. "Besides, as long as Tracy and Chris are in the game, we don't have a shot. Seriously, why would she go back on our alliance?"

"I don't know, but we better keep things close. Make sure David knows. We don't want this backfiring," Julia replies.

"Maybe you need to get your partner under control," Lucia quips. "I mean, if Vikki is going to screw us, she could be working your guy. You better nip that in the bud soon, mami. For all our sakes."

Julia nods her head before Lucia calls out to the men in the house that dinner is ready. Everyone makes their way into the kitchen and begins serving themselves as Julia looks on, wondering if her and Mitch's game plan is falling apart.

The next morning, Margie is at her desk working on a couple of items when an email notification pops up, grabbing her attention. She opens the email, which is from the station's legal department making her aware that Alexis has filed a suit against the show and its producers. Margie sighs before locking her computer and making her way to Dunbar's office. She knocks on the door as he waves her in with a big smile on his face.

"Hey, I've been reviewing the latest strategy room footage. This is great!" He exclaims, jubilated. "They are going to wait until the last possible moment before having sex with each other, and I need you to make it happen! I need them to last 'til the end. I know it's against your morals, but we can make this work. A campaign saying, 'Will they or won't they'! And if we're lucky, they will, and we'll have it all on film! This could be huge!"

"Sir, we can't broadcast sex on live TV," an irritated Margie responds. "I thought we've discussed that before. The FCC won't allow that."

"FCC? Have you seen what they let the networks get away with lately?" Dunbar quips. "Besides, it'll be tasteful. Nothing X-rated. The sex isn't the point. What's the point is the build up to it! I want them on each other's mind twenty-four seven. Make sure all future competitions have them interacting with each other as much as possible. I want their bodies pressed on each other as much as we can!"

Margie sighs and grabs her head with frustration.

"Sir, I just received an email from legal saying that Chris's wife has filed a suit against us," she informs. "As much as you're enjoying the ratings, I think it's time to seriously consider pulling these two. We can work the Victoria angle. Apparently, her and Mitch are rumored to have something going on, and I don't think she cares much about her husband on the outside. Mitch doesn't seem to care about his wife either. Chris's wife, however, isn't going to let this go."

"That's fine. Just have legal draw it out," Dunbar replies. "By the time this thing hits the courts, the season would be over. We can then settle out of court, or bleed them out. Either way, we're renewed for another season, and keep our jobs."

"But, sir, getting another season won't matter if everyone hears about this behind the scenes foolishness. Also, this is a onetime thing. You think any other contestants are going to fall for it in the future? I really think we need to talk to Mr. Brooks and see if he wants-"

"Mr. Brooks doesn't run this show, I do!" Dunbar snaps. "Now, I've made my decision! Make sure you keep this close and make sure those two are together as much as possible. We're going to milk this for all it's worth. At the end of this thing, I'll throw you a little something, as a thank you for making this happen."

Margie sighs before nodding her head. Dunbar rises from his chair and approaches his assistant with endearment in his eyes.

"I understand that this is hard for you. You have a good heart, Margie, and that's great. The thing is that this the entertainment world. If you're ever going to be something in this business, you're going to have to learn to put your feelings aside. This business is ruthless, and you have to be willing to do what needs to be done to get the only thing that matters, which are the ratings," Dunbar preaches. "It's not about what's right and what's wrong. It's about the numbers, and once you understand that, you'll do whatever it takes. Does that make sense?"

Margie is hesitant because while she believes that what Dunbar is doing is wrong, what he's saying isn't necessarily incorrect. It is a cutthroat business. If she ever wants to make it in the industry, she's going to have to develop nerves of steel in order to get to where she wants. She slowly nods her head in agreement, much to Dunbar's delight.

"Excellent!" He exclaims. "Trust me, you'll see. This will work out perfectly. It'll be our greatest achievement. Reality television at its finest."

Margie forces a smile on her face once more and nods her head before walking out of the office to carry out her boss's orders.

Chapter 11

Failed Alliances

A few days later, and several competitions later, Tracy and Chris are in a prime position leading the others by a hundred points. Julia and Mitch are second, Victoria and Sebastian are third, and Lucia and David are fourth. The teams are all lined up in the backyard wearing tight water suits and equipped with water guns. There are several other water firing devices lined up in the backyard as well as Melissa is explaining today's competition to the home audience. Chris tries to hide his glances as his team partner, who is fitting into her wet suit very nicely, accenting the curves on her body. Tracy takes a look at Chris occasionally to see his chiseled frame as well. Both are trying to go unnoticed while waiting further instructions.

"Okay, teams! There is a bunker at each of the four corners of the yard with your team number attached to them. The water battle will begin once you hear the sound of the horn. Once you're struck, you are out! We have several referees who will make the calls, so pay close attention! Good luck, ladies and gentlemen!"

Everyone nods their head and looks around for their bunkers. So far, Tracy and Victoria have kept their team's alliance hidden throughout the other events. Since this event will lead to another elimination day, Tracy and Chris decide it's time to enact their plan. Tracy makes eye contact and nods, letting Victoria know now is the time. Victoria smiles back and nods as well as all teams hide behind their assigned bunkers.

"I gave Vikki the sign," Tracy says as she readies her equipment. "So we attack the other two teams. No attack on Sebastian and her until the others are eliminated."

Chris looks back and her and smiles as the two catch a glimpse of each other once more.

"What?" Tracy asks.

"I mean, look at you. You weren't even a fan of the show, and now you're out here with secret alliances and plans," Chris points out, smirking. "Looks like you're all into it now."

"Well, I have a lot riding on it. There's a lot of money on the line," Tracy responds with a wink, also referencing their last night together plan, which meant more than the money to her. "You ready?"

Chris pumps up his water gun and nods.

"I was born ready," he replies, grinning.

The two teammates wait silently until the horn sounds. They both come out of their bunker and onto the field of play. Lucia and David run towards them firing, but are quickly taken out by the alliance as Sebastian, Victoria, Chris, and Tracy all attack them as one, drenching them.

"Fuck!" Lucia yells before the referee marks both she and David out.

Julia and Mitch notice the alliance from a distance and opt to take over one of the high-pressure water cannons located in the field. Mitch unleashes an attack on the other teams as

Julia covers him causing the others to take cover to avoid being struck. Mitch has the teams pinned down as they look at each other.

"They have the high ground! If movies have taught me anything, it's that once you have the high ground, it's over!" Sebastian yells.

"Shit! We're stuck! What are we gonna do?" Victoria asks, trying to keep her head out of harm's way.

Chris peeks from behind the barrier they were behind trying to get a lay of the land. After a few moments, he turns to the others as a plan forms.

"Look, they can't get all of us," he says. "I say we all go out at once and take our chances. We do it right. We should be able to take both of them."

"Man, that's suicide!" Sebastian responds. "As long as he has that thing, he can pluck us off one by one!"

"Not if Victoria goes first," Tracy replies, confusing the others.

"Me? Why?" Victoria asks.

"You know why," Tracy responds with a smirk. "Just draw his attention, and we'll try and do the rest. It's either that or sit here the whole day!"

After a few moments, Victoria agrees as she gets ready to run from cover.

"Alright, on my mark, we go. Try and make it to separate barriers!" Chris says as everyone nods their head, prepping to move. "Now!"

Victoria heads out first, drawing Mitch's attention. Just as Tracy thought, he doesn't immediately go after her causing the distraction the others needed to break away. A furious

Julia growls as she breaks cover as well, heading out with intentions on eliminating Victoria. The move leaves Mitch's back uncovered as Tracy and Chris quickly make their way around towards the water cannon's rear. They both open fire, attacking a stunned Mitch, wetting him up until a ref calls him out. Mitch is furious Julia left him exposed as she is called out after being outgunned by both Victoria and Sebastian. The two remaining teams look at each other with smiles on their faces. They both know this week they were safe based on the pact with each other.

After a few moments, the battle is on between the final two teams as Sebastian opens fire with his water gun, nearly tagging Tracy. Chris sets his sights on Victoria as he follows her towards the far end of the yard. Tracy takes on Sebastian, but the odds aren't in her favor as her gun runs out of water.

"Shit," she says before running for cover. Sebastian smiles as he unloads his gun at her, missing her with each squirt.

Victoria has fallen prey to Chris, who easily wets her up as she's out of breath running from him. She giggles as she walks off the battlefield, drenched. Tracy is cornered and is awaiting her fate as Sebastian walks up and realizes she had nowhere to go. He's about to unload on her when Chris sneaks up behind him to grab his attention.

"Hey. You ever danced with the devil on the pale moonlight?" Chris asks as he pumps up his gun.

Sebastian chuckles and nods his head. He quickly tries to turn around and shoot his rival but just misses Chris, who falls towards the ground. Chris unloads his weapon drenching his rival. Sebastian drops to his knees, mimicking the infamous Platoon Movie scene with his hands reaching towards the sky before collapsing on the ground as the referee calls him out. An excited Tracy runs over and helps Chris from the ground as the two start to celebrate.

"What a win! Chris and Tracy take the competition and maintains their hold on the top spot," Melissa says to the cameras as she walks over to interview the contest winners. "Chris, Tracy, what a performance. It seemed that Mitch and Julia had the upper hand there for a moment. How were you able to pull this victory off?"

"Just worked in our favor, I guess," Chris answers. "My teammate came up with the strategy, and we just executed, so I have to give her all the credit on this one."

"Tracy, it looked like Sebastian had you there for a moment. How did you feel when Chris got the better of him?" Melissa asks, turning the attention towards Tracy.

"Well, it's like having a knight in shining armor," Tracy answers, a phrase she always compared Chris to in the past. "I mean, sometimes we all need saving, so I'm glad it was him."

"Well, since you are the leading team, now's your chance to pick two teams who will go head to head in the elimination match here shortly. Which two teams will you have face off?" Melissa asks.

"We're going to nominate Julia and Mitch's team to go against Lucia and David's team," Tracy answers with a smile.

"Thank you, and again congratulations on your victory today," Melissa says before turning her attention back to the camera. "Up next, Julia and Mitch's team goes up against Lucia and David's team where the loser goes home. We'll be right back after these messages."

As soon as the cameraman yells clear, the smile on Melissa's face turns into a frown quickly as she approaches the gaffer production crew member.

"What the fuck? Are you trying to blind me?" She growls. "I'm over here trying to concentrate, and you're over here going 'da da da da da' with the fucking light!"

She continues to berate the lighting technician as Tracy and Chris make their way over and daps off their alliance teammates, much to Julia's displeasure, who is drying herself off. She tosses the towel off to the side and approaches Victoria in a blind rage.

"So, I see you're just as fast with your word as you are with these men!" She exclaims, catching everyone off guard. "I knew we shouldn't have trusted your ass!"

"Julia, calm down," Mitch says, trying to get in between the two women. "It's just a game. It's about-"

"Fuck that! You're no different than her!" Julia responds, turning her anger towards her partner. "You had her! She was directly in your line of sight, and you let her get away! I knew I shouldn't have trusted her, but I let you talk me into it because you and her had a connection, or whatever you want to call it! Can't believe I was that stupid! I hope that blow job she gave you was worth it because you probably cost us a million dollars!"

"Julia! That's enough," Tracy says as she steps in as well when she notices Victoria's feelings were hurt. "You're out of line!"

"No, it's cool, Tracy. It's fine," Victoria says before walking off back into the house.

Tracy looks at Julia as if she's ashamed of her before running back into the house to comfort her friend. Mitch tries to explain himself to his partner again but is rejected as Julia walks off to set up for the elimination event. Lucia, who is still drying herself off from the previous event, is livid over Victoria and Sebastian's betrayal as well. Julia joins her as both women have scowls on their faces.

"I should have listened to you," Lucia says, shaking her

head in disappointment. "I trusted that perra! I should have known better."

"Yeah. My idiot partner was no better," Julia responds, looking towards Mitch. "Never seen anyone fall like that. It's clear to me going forward I can't trust him dealing with anything Victoria related."

Julia takes a deep breath before pitching an idea to Lucia.

"Hey, I know we're going head to head on this thing. Whoever wins, the odds will be stacked against us. I heard from one of the production staff that next week they are going to do a partner swap competition with the women this time. Wouldn't it be nice if whoever wins that competition breaks up Chris and Tracy's royalty team? Think about it. Mitch clearly can't be trusted, and is David really that good?" Julia pitches, piquing Lucia's interest. "The only way we can win is by breaking them up. If I win this battle, it's exactly what I'm going to do. If you win, I suggest you think about doing the same. It's the only way you'll have a chance, trust me."

Lucia nods her head as she and Julia fist bump each other making their pact official.

"Consider it done, chica," Lucia says as the two women get themselves together for their elimination competition.

Back in the Team Experiment House, Tracy is sitting with Victoria in the women's bedroom trying to comfort her after Julia's remarks. Victoria is trying to wave it off but is clearly hurt by what was said.

"Look, don't trip on it," Tracy says. "Julia is all about winning, so she can't see past anything that hinders her. She was pissed off, but the game is the game. Hell, if we're lucky, she'll lose the next challenge and will be out of here."

"I get it. I really do. People say stuff all the time out of anger or whatever. I just... I don't know. If that exchange makes the show, how is it gonna look?" Victoria replies, her eyes watering up. "With my husband, I'm not too concerned about it because of the way we were before I got here, but Mitch has a wife and kids. He doesn't deserve this."

"I know, and it's all hearsay," Tracy replies, hinting that the cameras are still rolling. "Anytime a man and a woman are close, people start rumors. Julia being Julia, just shot her mouth off over things she doesn't know about. Her intention was to hurt and embarrass you."

"Mission accomplished," Victoria responds as tears start to run down her cheek. "I thought it would be fun to come here and compete, and hopefully win the money—a perfect start to my reality life. Maybe I shouldn't have acted the way I did. I don't know. I should have been better about all this."

Tracy smiles as she hugs her new friend to comfort her.

"Maybe we'll get lucky, and Lucia and David win," she says with a chuckle.

"You don't believe that yourself," Victoria replies, finally managing a smile.

A few moments later, as the two women talk with each other, Lucia bursts into the room and notices Tracy and Victoria sitting together. The room is silent as there is a stare down between all three ladies. Lucia frowns before making her way over to her bed and begins packing her things, signifying her team lost the competition. Tracy walks over and tries to comfort Lucia, but is quickly rejected.

"I don't need your pity," Lucia says while gathering her things. "You screwed me over, and it is what it is. It's all in the game, but it doesn't mean I gotta be all friendly about it."

Tracy nods her head and backs away as Lucia zips her bag

up. Just as she's about to walk out, Julia walks in and notices Lucia is all packed. She and Lucia share a brief hug before Lucia grabs her bag once again.

"Kick their asses," Lucia says before walking out of the room for the last time.

Julia nods her head before she looks towards Tracy and Victoria with a scowl still plastered on her face.

"And then there were two," she says before making her way out of the room.

Tracy and Victoria both look disappointed with the outcome. Still, they realize that the competition has now become real in the household.

Back in the WBC Network Office, Dunbar has just wrapped up a conference call in his office when Margie knocks on the door carrying a thumb drive. She takes a seat across from her boss, who is satisfied with the way things are working out thus far.

"Very dramatic competition yesterday," he said, smirking. "A lot of drama, and that's good. That Julia has amped things up. No more of this buddy nonsense. She wants to win, and the people are supporting her. Our final three teams are perfect for ratings."

"I assume you didn't review the footage I sent you earlier, so I brought it over to you because we might have a problem," Margie says as she hands Dunbar the thumb drive.

He inserts the drive into his computer and loads the video file that Margie is referring to. He watches the conversation between Lucia and Julia, making a pact to switch teams with Tracy if they won the event. The video disturbs Dunbar, and he quickly exits out of the footage.

"Well, that's no biggie. We can just nix the swap competition," Dunbar says, seemingly calm.

"Yeah, well the thing is that teasers have hit the air already hyping the swap event," Margie points out. "If we change it up now, folks will know the show is rigged. There's already a lot of talk via social media that we're rigging the show in Tracy and Chris's favor anyway, so just imagine what would happen if we made that move. You do realize what happens to shows that are supposed to be real, but end up being fake, right? Ask Jerry Springer how that worked out."

A frustrated Dunbar grabs his head as he tries to find a workaround.

"We can't let those two break apart!" He exclaims. "It's the baseline of the show! If they're not together, no strategy room diaries, if no strategy room diaries, no sleeping together, if no sleeping together, no ratings!"

Margie nods her head, but deep down inside, she's happy the way things are turning on her boss.

"What about the sexy one, Vikki?" Dunbar replies. "Any way we can get a win competition for her? Something that would throw the scent off of what we're trying to accomplish?"

"I mean, we probably could, but there was footage a while back with her saying she would switch if she got the chance to as well," Margie points out. "Although, that might have changed with how close her and Tracy have been lately. It's still a risk though."

"So maybe we offer her something she really wants in return," Dunbar mentions. "Like what would she take that would guarantee her not to choose to swap teams?"

After a few moments of thought, Dunbar snaps his fingers and smiles.

"I got the perfect thing!" He says with glee. "Make sure she wins the event. I'm gonna make her an offer she can't refuse."

Margie rolls her eyes at Dunbar's Godfather performance and is about to leave when Dunbar stops her.

"Hey. What's with this water fight nonsense?" He asks. "I thought I told you to turn up the heat between Tracy and Chris when it comes to the events. So far that's the only event I seen with any sex appeal, and neither one of them got wet."

"Sir, we're way over the event budget as it is. We paid for all these event props in advance, and none of them can be used as a sexual weapon for your pleasure. There's just no way to make it work," Margie pleas with her boss.

"Find a way, and make sure it's cheap," Dunbar says before waving Margie off.

Margie is stunned as she's trying to figure out how to stretch the budget even further to grant Dunbar's wish. After a few moments, she shakes her head and makes her way out the office, frustrated with everything being asked of her.

Chapter 12

The Final Four

The week has been a struggle for the Team Experiment contestants as several competitions have taken place, and all have been fierce. It's been especially difficult for Tracy and Chris as each challenge was designed to keep them close together. The first challenge was a pool chicken fighting challenge. The women were mounted on top of the men's shoulders, trying to push the other female contestants off their teammate into the water. Having Tracy mounted on him has Chris thinking about her since he was between her legs in the competition. Knowing she has him in that position drives Tracy wild as well as they end up losing the event to both teams.

The next competition was a wheel barrel race where the men are holding the women by their ankles and racing the other team as the women use their arms to move. Looking at Tracy's perfectly formed bottom catches Chris's attention as it jiggles with each movement she makes. Chris has a smirk on his face, but they did end up winning this event over the other two teams.

The last event is probably Margie's most blatant attempt to get the lovers thinking about each other in the 'Oil Me Up' competition. In this competition, the men stand poolside with nothing but their swimming trunks on as the women hurry to cover their bodies with tanning oil using only their hands. This challenge drives Tracy, especially wild, as she rubs oil all over her friend's body. When she reaches his abs, she is in heaven, slowing down to make sure she enjoys every rub. Chris also enjoys her touch as well. As much as the two enjoy their interaction, it costs them the challenge as once again, they came in last place.

After the oil challenge, Chris is wiping himself down with a towel when Tracy quickly approaches him. She has a lustful look in her eyes as she tries to keep her thoughts hidden for the moment.

"Hey, yeah, so I booked us some strategy room time. Let's go, cause I got something I need to talk about," she whispers to her lover.

"Okay, cool. Let me get dressed and-"

"No, we need to talk now," Tracy demands.

Chris can tell she wasn't taking no for an answer and nods his head before following her to the strategy room. As soon as the door closes, Tracy aggressively approaches Chris rubbing him on his abs once more, surprising her teammate. She's about to reach into his shorts when Chris quickly stops her.

"Damn, girl! What got into you?" He asks, backing away.

"I... I don't know," an equally confused, Tracy, responds. "I... these competitions lately have been getting to me, oh my God."

Chris sighs as he can relate.

"I'm not going to lie; it's been getting to me too," he says.

"I mean, who came up with this shit? I have to sit in a pool between your legs, then looking down at your sweet, perfect ass jiggle. I'm surprised I didn't get a hard-on for the world to see!"

"You?! Who in the hell comes up with an 'oil me up' competition?" Tracy fires back, causing her partner to laugh. "I'm serious! I'm like this is the most ridiculous thing I've ever seen, but when I touched your body... I... I couldn't help myself. I just wanted you so bad after that. I didn't know what to do. And yes, having you in between my thighs was tough on me too. Hard to concentrate when all I kept thinking was 'god, just let him turn around and work me over'."

After a few moments of sexual tension, the two lovers burst into laughter, stunned at what's going on. As they calm down, they both take a seat on the couch admiring each other. A smirk enters Tracy's face.

"So, you think I have a perfect ass?" She asks, referring to Chris's earlier comment.

"You always did. It's not too big, not too small. It's just right. For me anyway," Chris admits. "I'm not going to lie to you, I'm ready to dive right in right now. The problem is with all this temptation going on, we're in last place this week. Bottom two teams have no choice but to face off in an elimination match. We're only behind by seventy-five points, so we need to hit on this last competition, or that could be curtains for us."

"Then why don't we get it out of our system now so we can focus," Tracy suggests with a smile.

"You know why," Chris replies. "The whole reason we decided to wait was that you didn't want to feel the guilt while in the house."

"True, but if we lose tomorrow's event, and then the challenge after that, today is technically our last day in the house," Tracy points out. "Are we willing to risk it?"

Chris is unsure as he thinks silently for a moment. He wants nothing more than to agree with Tracy, but he knows that the show isn't over yet, and Tracy living with guilt could cost them the future winnings if they are able to survive the week. He takes a deep breath before responding to his teammate.

"No, I'm not," he says, disappointing Tracy. "I still think we have a shot at the money. I didn't think I'd get this far, but here we are. We still have Victoria and Sebastian on our side, so that leaves Julia and Mitch on the outside looking in."

"Maybe," Tracy responds. "You know this next challenge allows the women to swap partners at the end of it, right?"

"Wait, what?" A confused Chris inquires, hearing this for the first time. "But that doesn't make any sense to do it this late in the game."

"It's what I heard. If Julia wins, I wouldn't be surprised if she broke us up. Hell, not one hundred percent sure I trust Victoria. Only reason I think she'll let us make it is because she'll more than likely be leading the scoreboard and safe from elimination. Julia could do it out of spite. She's still pissed about that whole water fight thing."

Chis sighs, uncertain on how to feel with the news presented to him.

"Then we got to go out swinging. We need to win this late competition big," Chris says. "I can see the end is near. We're almost there! We need to put all this behind us for the moment and focus on the game. As much as I want to do you now, I really want to win that money. It's life changing."

A disappointed Tracy sighs, knowing her partner is right. Still, she wants a little something before they part ways.

"I'm with you, but in the meantime, can I... well, you

know," she says, smirking and motioning towards Chris's mid-section.

It takes him a second to catch on what she's requesting. Once he does, he gives her a slight nod.

"If you must," he responds with confidence.

An excited Tracy reaches over and goes into her partner's shorts and underwear to grasp on to Chris's manhood. With a blush, Tracy giggles to herself being able to feel her lover's shaft and takes a deep breath enjoying her touch.

"That should give you some motivation for tomorrow," Chris brags as Tracy removes her hand from his shorts.

"It's alright," Tracy plays off. "I mean, it's a little motivating, not win a million dollars motivating."

Chris shoots his partner a look, causing Tracy to burst into laughter. After a few moments, Tracy lays her head on Chris's shoulder, wondering what the future holds for the two.

The next day, all three remaining teams are sitting outside in the back yard once again as Melissa is readying herself to speak on camera. Tracy looks towards Julia, who shoots her a scowl before turning her attention towards Melissa.

"Welcome back, ladies and gentlemen," Melissa greets, looking into the camera. "It's elimination day, but before we can get to that, we need to see what two teams will be battling it out by having one final competition. When we first started, our first competition had the option for the male winner, who happened to be Chris, swap teammates if he so chose. He did, adding Tracy to his team, and while they've struggled to get things going this week, it's worked out pretty well for him. This challenge, we're going to give the ladies the opportunity to make that same call. The winner of this competition will have the ability to swap partners. Unlike Chris, however, you're going to have to make your decision right after the competition."

A smirk enters Julia's face as this is what she's been waiting for. Not only would she get a chance to break Tracy and Chris up, but she would have a chance to pair up Mitch, who she considers as a liability to Tracy, making them the weaker team in her mind.

"That being said, fellas, you deserve some time off. Take a seat in the lounging area," Melissa instructs.

Chris and the other males all take a seat at the lounging area to watch the competition from the deck. Melissa turns her attention to the females who are anxiously awaiting the next competition.

"Okay, ladies, we decided the last competition should be something that shows your skills in long-range combat," Melissa teases as it's revealed that the final contest is an archery contest.

Victoria's eyes light up with excitement as Melissa explains the rules.

"Today, you will compete in an archery contest to earn points for the event," Melissa says. "As you can see, marked on the ground are three shooting points. The closest one is one hundred points, the second one is two hundred points, and the third one is three hundred points. You each will get three shots to hit the target. Now, you only have to hit the target to earn the line's points, but if you are able to hit the bullseye, we will add an additional one hundred points to your score. You can choose to shoot at any line on the ground, but remember, you only have three shots, so make it count."

An overjoyed Victoria can't wait till it's her turn. Melissa walks over to Tracy first, who is given a bow and three arrows by one of the production staff.

"Tracy, since your team is in last place, you get to go first. Can you describe your comfort level with shooting a bow?" Melissa asks.

"I'd have to say a one, seeing as I've never held a bow in my life," Tracy admits as she tries out the bow.

"Okay, one of the crew will give you quick instructions to get you started," Melissa explains as Tracy is waved over by one of the crew members.

"Will Tracy be able to add points on the board? We'll find out after this short break."

Once the camera yells cute, Chris runs over to Tracy, who is getting a quick lesson.

"Hey, I say play it safe," he says to her after the crew member walks off. "Just take all three shots at the one hundred point line. All you need to do is hit the target."

"Yeah, that's what I was thinking too," Tracy says as she practices what the crew member taught her. "Wish me luck."

"You got this," Chris responds before making his way back to the lounging area.

Tracy takes her position next to Melissa as the show returns from commercial break.

"Welcome back! Tracy has had instructions, and ready to make her first attempt to gain her team some much needed points. Tracy, whenever you're ready," Melissa says.

Tracy takes a deep breath before walking over to the one hundred point line. She follows the brief instructions she received to the best of her ability as she aims for the target. Her first shot falls short as her arrow digs into the grass. Her second attempt hits the edge of the target earning her and Chris one hundred points, exciting her. She takes a deep breath as she aims her final shot and releases. It also hits the target, earning another hundred points. Tracy smiles and does a little dance, excited with her results.

"Nice shooting, Tex," Melissa says to Tracy. "With that, you and Chris have taken a slight lead! Way to go!"

Tracy bows to everyone before making her way to the lounging area. She hi-fives Chris as Julia is up next in the competition. Julia decides to try her first shot from the three hundred point line, trying to quickly end the competition. She misses horribly, overestimating her newly learned skills. She moves to the two hundred line for her second shot, just missing the mark, grunting in disappointment. Knowing Tracy added two hundred points for her team, Julia has no choice but to try once again at the two hundred point line to offset her gains and take the overall lead. She lines up the shot as best she can, and was able to just hit the target, fist-pumping after the strike.

"Unbelievable!" Melissa exclaims. "Julia has hit the target from the two hundred point line, which not only gives them the overall lead. It puts Tracy and Chris automatically into the elimination match if the teams stay as they are."

Julia walks over with a smug smile as she daps off Mitch. Tracy and Chris look worried as Victoria is next up.

"Alright, Victoria. You're down one hundred and fifty points. You have three shots to get two hundred points to take the lead and send Julia and Mitch into the elimination round. Good luck," Melissa says.

"Don't worry. I just need one shot," a confident Victoria says as she makes her way well beyond the three hundred point line.

She aims her bow as if she's a professional, making sure to aim just above the target taking account for height, distance, and wind resistance. She takes a deep breath and fires her arrow while exhaling. Her arrow hits the bull's eye stunning the rest of the contestants and Melissa. She flips the bow forward, and struts with a cocky walk as she makes her way over to an astonished Melissa.

"I'm going to go out on a limb here and say this isn't your first time using a bow and arrow," Melissa deduces.

"No. I competed back in high school. Had a couple of first place finishes to my name," a smiling Victoria admits. "Once I saw what we were doing, I knew it was over!"

"Well, the luck of the draw has given you and Sebastian the advantage as you are now safe from elimination as it currently stands," Melissa informs. "The question is will you keep your partner Sebastian, or will you swap him for Chris or Mitch?"

Victoria looks over towards the lounging area and looks as though she's conflicted. Before she announces her decision, Melissa cuts her off.

"Now, before you say anything, I have a special offer for you," she says, piquing Victoria's interest. "You have the choice of either swapping partners today, or you can opt to be on the new reality show Texas Housewives, which premieres this fall. We left one slot open just for such an occasion."

Victoria is overwhelmed with joy as the decision is easy for her.

"Oh, I want to be on the show!" She responds excitedly.

"Is that your final answer?" Melissa inquires.

Victoria nods her head as Melissa turns to the camera.

"Well, you're looking at Texas Housewives' newest member," Melissa announces. "Congratulations on winning today's event."

A spirited Victoria runs off to the side celebrating as she jumps into Sebastian's arms as he tries to meet her.

"Coming up, Tracy and Chris battle it out with Julia and Mitch to see who stays, and who goes on today's edition of Team Experiment," Melissa says before the camera cuts the feed.

In the lounge, Victoria is still celebrating as she walks over and hugs Tracy.

"Oh my god, I'm gonna be a housewife!" She exclaims.

"That's cool," a bewildered Tracy responds. "But don't you work?"

"I won't if we win this thing," Victoria fires back with a smile. "Even if we don't, from what I can get paid for doing that show, it's not gonna matter."

Victoria hugs Tracy once more, still overwhelmed with excitement when Julia makes her way over with a frown filling her face.

"Congratulations. It seems luck just seemed to fall in your favor," a sarcastic Julia responds. "We just so happen to compete in a challenge in a field that you were trained for. I mean, what are the odds? Seriously."

Tracy has heard enough as she steps in between Julia and Victoria.

"You know what? I've had enough of your bullying!" Tracy replies. "Don't get mad because she won an event. If you had won, we wouldn't be hearing any of this."

"Bullshit," Julia fires back. "You have to see they are fixing this show for who they want to win. I mean, it's just as obvious when they fixed the trivia game for you that sent Monica and Gerald home. It's like they want you and Chris to win. It doesn't matter though. No matter what, I'm going to send you and your boyfriend home today. This much, I promise."

"He's not my boyfriend. He's my teammate," Tracy corrects, causing Julia to smile.

"I'm sure he is. Ever since you became good friends with the house slut, it seems you've started taking on a few of her whorish qualities," Julia responds, enraging Tracy.

Tracy is about to attack Julia when Victoria pulls her away, struggling to hold her back. Tracy and Julia continue to go back and forth until the men jump in and quickly pull them apart. Melissa motions to the cameraman to get some shots of the dispute, loving the altercation between the two. Tracy is finally led away by Chris and Victoria as they try to calm down their friend.

"Tracy, calm down. It's not that serious," Chris says.

"I'm sick of her shit!" Tracy exclaims. "Somebody needs to teach that bitch a lesson!"

"Then do it at the competition!" Chris responds, trying rally his friend. "Take from her the thing she loves the most. Send her ass packing. You want to come out on top of this thing? Send her ass home!"

An enraged Tracy looks over towards Julia and notices the smug smirk on her face looking back at her. She gets her emotions in check and nods her head.

"I got this," she says. "Let's do this."

Chris smiles and nods his head as well, as the production crew are calling the competitors to stand next to Melissa. Before Tracy walks off, Victoria pulls her to the side.

"Good luck. Spank her ass for me," she said, smirking.

Tracy smiles and daps her friend off before joining the competing teams next to Melissa. Tracy and Julia have a brief stare down during the countdown to return to air.

"We're back, ladies and gentlemen, to our elimination challenge!" Melissa says. "It's been a battle, to say the least, this season. It all started after the first competition when Chris decided to switch partners adding Tracy to his team. Let's watch how we got to where we are today."

The screen located in the yard starts playing highlights from their first competition as Tracy and Julia continue to stare down each other. Chris smiles when he sees the replay of Tracy purposely sabotaging the first event and thinks back to when he first saw her that day. He never thought he'd see her again and was stunned to be in her presence. He glances at her with a small smirk, wishing he could hug her right then and there. As the video highlights end, it's revealed that two platforms are set up in the back yard for an old traditional challenge.

"As you can see, these two teams have had quite a battle to get this far. We thought it would only be fitting to bring back Team Experiment's oldest and most popular challenge, the platform," Melissa reveals as the teams look towards the setup. "As always, gentlemen, it will be your challenge to hold your team up figuratively and literally. You will stand on the platform holding your female counterparts for as long as you can. Ladies, if any of your body parts touch the platform, your team is immediately eliminated. Fellas, if anything but your feet touches the platform, your team is immediately eliminated. This is a test of endurance and strength. The team who last the longest will win the event and head off into the finals to face Victoria and Sebastian. Does everyone understand the rules?"

All competing contestants nod their heads as they are led to their separate platforms by crew members. Melissa smiles as she turns her attention towards the camera.

"We will stick around as long as we can, but just in case these two teams are still holding strong by the end of the hour, you can continue to catch the live feed by visiting the Team Experiment website," she explains.

While she's giving out the website to the viewers, Tracy and Chris step on to their platform which is risen about five feet from the ground and is very narrow for two people.

"So, what's the best way to do this?" Tracy asks her partner. "I'm assuming you've seen this before, being a fan and all."

"Yeah, most women get on their partner's back and wrap their legs around their waist to help relieve some weight," Chris responds as he carefully positions himself in the middle of the platform. "Others face each other with the same position only the opposite way. Honestly, I don't think there is one solid way to do this. I've seen folks win multiple ways."

"Alright, so how you want to do it then?" Tracy asks.

"Let's go the piggyback method. We can switch if we need to, and that's probably the best position to start from," Chris answers.

Tracy nods her head as she looks towards Mitch and Julia, who are also discussing their options. Melissa turns to the teams and approaches them from below.

"Okay, teams, are you ready to get this started?" She asks.

Both teams give the thumbs up.

"Okay, on your march, get set, go!" Melissa yells as both Tracy and Julia hop onto their partner's back.

Julia and Tracy try to balance their weight as best they can in order to take some pressure off of Chris and Mitch. Both men are standing comfortably for the moment, making sure to maintain their balance on the narrow platform. Margie is watching from the dining room area in the Team Experiment House when her cell phone suddenly rings. She rolls her eyes when she notices that Dunbar is calling her.

"Yes, sir," she answers, already knowing what he was calling for.

"Margie, what are you doing?" He yells. "Why did you break out the platform?"

"Because, sir, we use it once a season, and we hadn't done it yet this season. You know how it goes," a smug Margie answers.

"I told you to fix it so that Chris and Tracy make it to the finals! You could have used this platform challenge next week!" Dunbar yells. "They could lose this thing, and our finale reveal could be ruined!"

"Sir, like I told you, people were already questioning if we were fixing the show. I gave the world a challenge to prove that we're on the up and up," Margie explains. "If they lose, then we can go with the rival storyline with Victoria versus Julia, which is showing good tracking as well."

"The entire season has been about Tracy and Chris! Not Julia and Victoria!" Dunbar yells. "You better hope they pull this out, or you'll be looking for another job by the end of the day!"

Dunbar abruptly hangs up the phone causing Markie to sigh. After a few moments, a slight grin enters her face, enjoying the trueness of the competition for the first time this season. She turns her attention back to the platform area and gets comfortable in her chair.

About an hour has gone by as the sun is starting to set. The camera crew is still filming the weary contestants who are starting to show fatigue. Chris's legs begin to wobble a bit as Tracy tries to reposition to balance him off. Mitch is also struggling to maintain his posture with Julia trying to keep him going with commands and orders. Tracy sighs as she whispers in her teammate's ear.

"Hey, how you holding up?" She asks, choosing to make a different approach than what Julia was doing.

"I... I don't know how much longer I can go," Chris admits, feeling weak. "This is killing me right now."

"You got this, Chris. I know you do," Tracy responds. "Just focus. Just keep your focus."

Chris sighs as he tries to maintain his strength. He looks over towards Mitch, hoping he would falter first, but neither man is willing to give up. Chris tries to concentrate as his partner instructs him, hoping to take his mind off the fatigue.

Another thirty minutes have gone by in this unprecedented display of stamina, which still has Mitch and Chris fighting to stay alive in the competition. Chris is on his last leg as he's starting to break down. Tracy notices and tries to motivate him once more.

"Hey, hey, settle down," she whispers. "We're going to make it."

"I... I... I don't think I can," a worn-out Chris says as his legs begin to buckle.

Tracy senses her partner is about to give, and quickly repositions herself to the front of Chris, catching him off guard, and almost sending him tumbling off the pedestal. She's now facing Chris, looking at him eye to eye. She can see her teammate starting to fade and does her best to comfort him.

"Look at me, Chris," she says. "Look in my eyes. You know what we have at stake here. You know it. Are you willing to throw in the towel? If you are, then do it, but remember what you're fighting for. Remember what's waiting for us at the end."

The inspirational speech starts to work on Chris, which allows him to strengthen up a bit. Tracy continues to repeat her words, hinting to him about their possible sexual connection that they agreed upon. While the money was definitely a motivating factor to Chris, the hope of lying with Tracy one last time meant more. It gave him the strength to carry on as he leans back slightly to balance Tracy's weight. Mitch is drenched with sweat as he begins to buckle under pressure. Julia looks over and Chris and is stunned to see how well Chris is holding up. She looks towards Mitch, who begins to shake.

"Don't you do this to me!" She exclaims. "Don't you let them win!"

"I... I can't hold it much longer," Mitch gasps. "I... I don't know."

Julia, trying to mimic Tracy, tries to reposition herself to Mitch's front to give his back some relief. The movement, however, is too much for Mitch. He tumbles over, sending both he and Julia falling onto the safety construct below the platform. A rage-filled Julia screams in fury, upset that she and Mitch have lost the event. She looks back towards Tracy and Chris, who are still in their position on the platform. The two are in their own world as the love they have for each other keeps them going, unaware that they've won the event. Chris wants to kiss his partner so bad but knows the cameras are still running. It isn't until Victoria runs up to the platform that they realize the event was over.

"Hey, guys! You won! You won!" An excited Victoria exclaims, severing the two lover's connection with each other.

Tracy slowly steps onto the platform and catches an exhausted Chris before he tumbled to the ground.

"We did it," she said with a smile on her face.

"Nah, you did it," Chris replies as the two daps each other.

The teammates slowly make their way off the platform and are met by Victoria and Sebastian, who congratulate them on their win. An angered Julia walks off, leaving her partner Mitch on the ground without trying to console him. Chris and the others walk over to Mitch and help him to his feet. They all congratulate him on a good challenge and hug him as a sign of respect. Victoria is the last to hug Mitch as there is some sadness to see her undercover lover leave the show. After several moments, everyone makes their way back into the house, getting prepped for the final week of competition.

Chapter 13

Game Over

Social media is ablaze as everyone is wondering will Chris and Tracy hook up their last night together in the Team Experiment House. It's the number one trending topic that has even talk shows and newscasts discussing it. There has also been some negative press as well, with Alexis leading a movement to protest the show claiming the show is holding Chris hostage for profit. There is noise everywhere as the final night is upon the couple. Throughout the week, during various competitions, Victoria and Sebastian have a slight fifty-point lead, which gives them the advantage going into the final event tomorrow. With all the noise in the world that's buzzing about the show, the only quiet place is the Team Experiment House.

The four remaining contestants are in the backyard gathered around a bonfire enjoying the sunset from the house for one last time. Unlike when Julia was there, the two teams get along well. They are enjoying each other's company with a breeze making the weather feel just perfect.

"I swear I'm gonna miss this shit," Victoria replies, looking around the yard. "I mean, this weather is perfect. Beautiful sunsets and I'm sure the beaches are life too. Makes me wanna relocate."

"Yeah, and you'll be heading right back to Texas once you see what the cost of living is out here," Sebastian responds with a chuckle. "Life out here costs. That's why it's so beautiful. If it cost the same as back home, this place would be well overpopulated."

"Shit, it's overpopulated already," Victoria points out. "Whatever it costs, I'm gonna make this home one day. You can bet that."

Sebastian chuckles as Victoria turns her attention towards Tracy and Chris, who are being especially quiet.

"What's up, you two?" Victoria asks, grabbing their attention. "Why are you so quiet over there?"

"I... I don't know. I guess, and I hate to say it, but I'm going to miss this place," Tracy admits. "I didn't even want to come here. My husband basically forced me to. This was a dream of his, and here I am, living his dream. You're right, though. It is nice out here. The weather and... everything's just perfect."

Victoria can tell that her friend is a little distracted and can guess the reason why. She rises and pulls Tracy up as well, confusing her.

"Let's have a little girl talk," Victoria says as she leads Tracy to the dead zone area outside of the house. Sebastian looks on, confused.

"What's that all about?" He asks Chris.

"It's women. There's never a logical reason to anything they do," Chris fires back, causing Sebastian to laugh.

Chris continues drinking his beer in deep thought as well, wondering if anything is happening that night between him and his partner.

Victoria is as giddy as a schoolgirl as she and Tracy arrive at the dead zone.

"So, are you going to do it?" Victoria asks.

"Do what?" Tracy replies, acting as though she doesn't know what her friend is referring to.

"Don't play games with me. I know you're thinking long and hard about sleeping with Chris," Victoria says, reading her friend's face. "I think you both waited until this day to do it. Tell me I'm lying."

Tracy has a horrible poker face, covering her face with embarrassment.

"Oh my god, is it that obvious?" She asks.

"Girl, please. This last week I've been watching y'all two. I can see it. You all but told me about it when we last met," Victoria responds with a smile. "The question is, are you gonna go through with it?"

Tracy hesitates as she's still unsure of her feelings on the subject.

"Honestly, I don't know," Tracy admits. "I keep thinking about his wife, his son, and... I mean, it's his family that's really stuck in my mind."

"Whatever he's not getting from her, clearly you have it," Victoria points out. "Look, I don't know his history or background, but just like me and Mitch, there are some things we both weren't getting. It can be just as easy as lust, but whatever it is, you might as well get it out of your system while you can. Tonight is the last night you'll have the chance. Tomorrow, it'll be too late. You don't wanna regret this for the rest of your life."

Tracy sighs as she knows Victoria is speaking the truth. Still, Chris's family weighs heavily on her thoughts still, causing a sense of guilt.

"Why don't you and Chris get some strategy time in?" Victoria says with a smirk. "Don't worry, I'll keep Sebastian in the dark. Just don't make too much noise in there."

Tracy giggles as she and Victoria make their way out of the dead zone area and back towards the bonfire next to their partners.

Back at the WBC headquarters, Margie is packing her things up for the night, getting ready to head home when Dunbar notices her walking back from the break room.

"Where do you think you're going?" He asks his assistant, checking the time on a nearby clock. "The season finale is tomorrow. I'd think you'd be overseeing everything to make sure we're ready to go."

"Everything is planned as it should be," Margie answers. "The final challenge will be constructed overnight, and the streaming platform is on watch for your expected televised porno. I, however, won't be in until later in the day tomorrow. I have a meeting with Mr. Brooks in the morning, and depending on how long that takes, I probably won't be available until the beginning of the shoot."

News of Margie's meeting with Brooks startles Dunbar as he looks for clarity.

"Meeting with Mr. Brooks? Meeting about what?" He inquires.

"Can't say for sure, sir. He's not too pleased with this whole protest going on being led by Chris's wife. She's made a lot of noise out there that makes the show, and by extension, the network, look bad," Margie informs. "He's probably doing an investigation on anything immoral that went on with the show, or something like that. Anyway, I'll see you later, boss."

"Whoa, just a second," Dunbar says, blocking his assistant's path. "I know we've made some decisions that weren't exactly on the up and up. I don't think-"

"*We've made some decisions?*" Margie responds, cutting off Dunbar. "Let the record show that I didn't make any decisions in regards to the whole Chris and Tracy saga. I told you not to run with that angle, but did you listen? No. I told you to pull them once we found out they had a history. I even told you to pull Chris when his wife came to us looking for answers. All you could see is the ratings. That's all any of you could see. Mr. Brooks went along with it too because he sees the numbers just like you, and that's it. He's probably only now looking into it because he, just like you, didn't think Chris's wife could make as much noise as she did."

"This is the business, Margie. We're are in the business to get people to watch no matter the cost!" Dunbar exclaims. "They wanted the numbers, and I got it for them! They wanted compelling storylines and I created it! This is fucking Emmy winning television! The whole world is watching what happens tonight! Why can't you see that?!"

Margie chuckles and shakes her head, seeing that her boss is drunk with ratings power.

"You sold your soul for the numbers," she reminds him. "And now that it backfired, the network is probably looking for a scapegoat. Me? I'm small potatoes. Not worth firing. They are probably looking for a big name executive to take the fall. Wonder who falls into that category?"

Dunbar is speechless as Margie checks the time on her cell phone.

"Well, I guess I'll see you later, boss," she says before making her way out of the office, grinning.

A stunned and nervous Dunbar is in disbelief with Margie's reveal and is now wondering if he went too far with his show decisions.

Later that night, back in the Team Experiment House's Strategy Room, Chris and Tracy walk into the room for the last time. There is tension in the air as the two lovers know what's at stake for the night and are unsure of their intentions thus far. Chris shuts the door and looks at his friend with admiration. He can tell that Tracy is nervous and didn't' want to put any extra pressure on her to make a decision that's going to follow them for the rest of their lives. Tracy starts to giggle as a thought hits her mind.

"It's funny. I don't know why this is so hard," she says. "I remember back at the cell shop when we did what we did, it just kind of happened, you know. I didn't come in that day planning it out. It just happened casually. For the past few weeks though, I've been going through this day over and over in my head. Quite honestly, I didn't think we'd make it this far. Now that we're here, it's like I don't know what to do."

Chris nods his head, understanding the struggle she's going through as he leads her over to their familiar couch and takes a seat.

"Yeah, it's one thing when it just happens. It's an entirely different thing when it's planned out," he admits. "I've been going back and forth with it too. The first time was special. Here was the girl I had a little thing, who was the sole reason I stayed at the job as long as I did telling me at the last possible moment that she's leaving my life for good."

"I tried to tell you a couple of times prior, but I didn't know how to say it," Tracy admits. "I had been looking for a job for a couple of weeks. When it was offered, I was so happy to be finally out of that damn place. Then it hit me when I came in one morning that I wouldn't see you again. It was rough, believe me."

Both friends get comfortable on the couch as they reminisce with each other. Tracy lays her head on Chris's chest with a smile on her face, thinking about their first time.

"All I could think about is this is it. This loving, caring guy who helped me make quota I don't know how many times was going to be out of my life forever," Tracy continues. "I knew if I didn't tell you how I really felt, I would regret it for the rest of my life."

"Yeah, I was a little shocked that you felt the same way I did," Chris admits. "With all the things I was going through at home, I guess I created this whole fantasized view of you. Of us. You were the exact opposite of my wife, and that's what made you so attractive."

"And you were the exact opposite of my husband," Tracy points out. "And I just remember thinking if I don't do this, I'd never forgive myself. I just threw it out there and hoped you wouldn't reject me."

"And here we are, years later. So I guess my question to you is, what's changed?" Chris asks.

Not knowing how to respond to Chris's question, Tracy remains silent, still thinking about their first time. She's trying to convince herself that there's nothing wrong wanting sex from her friend, but the thoughts of his family still crept into her head.

"What changed is your family," Tracy admits as she lifts her head from her lover's chest, looking at him deep into his eyes. "That last time was a spur of the moment type of thing. I wasn't thinking straight, and when it hit me, it hit me hard. At that exact moment, there was nothing else that mattered. This time, I've had a lot of time to think. Even in my shitty marriage, what we did was wrong. It was wrong then, and it's wrong now."

"So, are you saying we're not going to do this?" Chris inquires, seeking confirmation.

Tracy hesitates to answer as she still wants Chris with every ounce of her soul. In her mind, the only two people in the world who would ever know about it would be her and Chris. She looks at him and smiles.

"Why do I have to decide this?" She asks. "I mean, you're involved too. What are your thoughts on it?"

Chris takes a deep breath before sharing his thoughts.

"I'm not going to lie; these events the past couple of weeks has had you on my mind," Chris admits. "The elimination event against Julia and Mitch, I was ready to throw in the towel. My body had been battered and I was done. I didn't have anything else to give. That was until you reminded me what I was fighting for. Just the thought of this moment right here motivated me to get through it all. Without that, we'd be at home watching the rest of the show unfold. You were my strength at a time when I was weak. It's not just about the sex either. It's about how I feel about you as a person. I... I love you."

A stunned Tracy slowly backs away as the two sit upright on the couch. She shakes her head in disbelief, refusing to allow Chris to get to her.

"You... you can't love me. You just can't," she says, feeling overwhelmed. "You're married. I'm married. We can't have this conversation."

"Yes we can," Chris affirms. "I think the only reason this is making you nervous is because you feel the same way. You don't love your husband. You love me. I don't love my wife. I love you. These are facts, and you're too scared to face them."

Tracy jumps up from the couch and slowly backs away. She's about to head towards the door when Chris jumps up and stops her from leaving. Tracy is shaking her head as her emotions begin to catch up to her.

"Tracy. Look at me! Please, look at me," Chris says.

Tracy slowly turns around and faces her lover with a few tears streaming from her face.

"Tell me you don't love me, and I'll step back and leave all this alone," Chris says. "You want this to end, just say it now, and I'll never bring it up again."

Tracy is silent as the world watches on the edge of their seats, wondering how she's going to respond. She looks away from Chris in sadness, which lets him down. He's about to back away when Tracy finally makes eye contact with him.

"Aw, the hell with it," she said, mimicking her exact phrase from their first sexual encounter.

She moved in and kisses Chris passionately, setting up the mood for the two lovers. The red glare from the lights fills their body as Chris kisses Tracy on her neck, getting her going. He continues to work on her body driving Tracy wild before they make their way back towards the couch. Tracy begins to unbuckle her lover's pants as Chris hikes up her dress and removes her panties. The two are about to go at it when Tracy suddenly stops Chris's advances. While what Victoria said to her echoed in her head, she still couldn't bring herself to make the mistake she made all those years ago again. The guilt still weighs heavily on her, as she jumps up and grabs her panties from the floor.

"I'm sorry, Chris. I can't," a tearful Tracy says as she heads out of the room, leaving Chris disappointed.

He sighs as she buttons his pants back up and sits silently for several moments. Although he is frustrated with her decision, he still respects her for making the choice he wasn't able to make. He realizes she's doing what's right, and even though he wanted her, he agrees with her stance. After a few moments of silence, he sighs before making his way out of the room and back to the male bedroom.

Margie, who was in her bed watching the live feed from her cell phone, smiles when she sees the results. She had hoped they'd do the right thing all along and was ecstatic to see the results. She checked multiple social media sites to see the reaction and was pleasantly surprised to see how many people were rooting for the couple not to go through with it. Some were vilifying Chris for not thinking of his wife and kids. Others argue that Tracy was the problem being the aggressor of the interaction. Still, there was a positive buzz throughout social media, which warms Margie's heart before she decides to turn in for the night.

The final challenge has been set as both teams walk into the back yard to see a huge obstacle course set up filling the area. They are at awe with the construct that's equipped with a mud pit, a hill with a reverse escalator attached, a high platform with a zip line to the ground, a basketball hoop, and a swimming lane in the pool among other things. As the teams look over the course, Melissa walks over and quickly grabs their attention.

"Okay, guys. I'm gonna go over this once, so pay attention," she says to them. "The course starts right there in the far corner. It's all in a circle, but if you get confused about where to go next, just follow the arrows on the ground to the next area. Mitch and Julia, you have the lead, so you'll get ten seconds deducted from your time automatically. Pay special attention to the basketball hoop. You have five shots. For each shot you make, you get five seconds off your time. You've signed waivers, so if you get injured, it's on you. It's a tag-team event. The ladies will start off, and once they pass the finish line, the men will start in. Victoria, you and Sebastian are up first. Any questions?"

Sebastian raises his hand but is ignored by Melissa.

"Okay, thank you. Let's get lined up so we can get this going," she says.

The confused teams are positioned by the crew as the countdown to go live begins. Chris looks at Tracy and smiles with confidence as he nods his head to her. They haven't spoken much since the strategy room meeting but were ready to put their best foot forward to win this prize money. Melissa greets the viewers, reminding them that this was the show's finale, and explaining the course to them, much better than she did with the contestants. When it was all said and done, Tracy and Chris were sent to the lounge area to watch their rivals take on the course.

Watching from inside the Team Experiment House is Margie keeping an eye over the day's final events. As Victoria takes off starting the obstacle course, Margie receives a call on her cell phone.

"Hello," she answers, keeping an eye on Victoria, who is in the mud pit.

"Margie, hi," Mr. Brooks says, stunning her. "I hope this isn't a bad time."

"Oh, no, Mr. Brooks. I was just at the house making sure everything is working as planned," Margie responds, walking away from the window and quickly heading into the strategy room for more privacy. "Is everything okay?"

"Yes. Thanks to you," Mr. Books responds. "I want to

thank you for your help in the investigation this morning. I met with the board, and as of an hour ago, Dunbar has been relieved from his duties. We'll make a statement shortly in that regard. I was hoping to make another decision about your future as well."

Margie tenses up, not knowing where the studio head is going with the conversation.

"My future?" A timid Margie asks.

"Yes. I know things weren't as we thought they'd be, and I'll admit, the numbers made us overlook certain aspects of the show's events. What we need is someone with your moral code to develop the Team Experiment Brand going forward. That being said, we'd like to offer you a seat at the executive table with full control over the next season of Team Experiment."

Margie is speechless as her heart is filled with joy, surprised to have been chosen to take her boss's spot.

"We're having a board meeting in the next hour. I know it's last minute, and you have a lot going on, but I'd sure like to introduce you to the rest of the board in that meeting. Assuming you accept the position, of course," Mr. Brooks continues, awaiting a response from the former assistant.

"Oh, yes. I mean, I accept, and yes, I'd love to come to the meeting," Margie responds as if she's calm. "I don't know what the traffic is looking like, but I'm on my way. Thank you, Mr. Brooks. You have no idea what this means to me!"

"It's well deserved. Well deserved. Anyway, I'll see you in a little bit," Mr. Brooks says before hanging up the line.

Margie screams out in joy before calming down, realizing the room is still wired for sound and video. She quickly exits the room and grabs her things before hustling out of the house into her car, heading to the network.

Back at the competition in the back yard, Sebastian just finished his run on the obstacle course. He and Victoria, who are both sweaty and muddy from their run, embrace each other exhausted. Melissa walks over towards them, clapping but making sure she keeps her distance to avoid staining her outfit.

"Sebastian, Victoria, that was a remarkable run. You both ended with a time of six minutes and fifty-four seconds," she says, congratulating the team. "Well, you've certainly made it hard for Tracy and Chris. Do you feel that money is yours?"

"I don't know about all that, but what I do know is that me and my partner put it all on the line," Sebastian said, hugging his partner once more.

"Well, when we come back, Tracy and Chris will get their turn in the obstacle course for a chance to win one million dollars. Stay tuned for the final competition run on Team Experiment!" Melissa says to the camera before they go on a commercial break.

Tracy and Chris make their way over to the starting position, trying to focus on the task at hand. The benefit of them going second allowed them to see the course and the challenges the competitors went through first.

"Alright, that's a tight time to beat," Chris admits. "We need to make up ground somewhere. My guess is going to be the hoops challenge. We need to really make those shots. I don't suppose you've played in the WNBA or anything?"

Tracy looks at Chris strangely as his joke falls flat on her.

"Don't worry, I got this," she said as she strapped on her safety helmet. "Just be ready to blast out of here when I come around."

Chris nods his head as the two lovers look at each other

once more. A thousand thoughts are running through their heads as Tracy takes a deep breath prepping for her competition.

"Hey, Chris, listen. About what we talked about last night. I just want to-"

"I understand. Thank you. I appreciate it," he replies with a smile filling his face. "Now, go take care of this and win me my money."

Tracy giggles before she and her partner share a quick hug. As the show comes back from break, Melissa welcomes the viewers back as shots of Tracy and Chris fill the big screens. They add ten seconds on the clock to give Victoria and Sebastian their advantage before counting down for Tracy to begin. As the buzzer sounds, Tracy shoots off and starts making her way through to course, first diving into the pool and swimming onto the other side. The next obstacle is the mud pit, which she has to crawl through to get to the other side. In the distance, Chris is cheering for her as she quickly climbs up the lifted platform. She's met by one of the crew members, who hooks her to the zip line that sends her back down to the ground onto the basketball set up. Much to Chris's surprise, Tracy hits all five of her shots, which earns their team twenty-five seconds off their overall time. The next obstacle, the reverse escalator hill climb, gives Tracy trouble as she's starting to run out of gas. She finally makes it to the top and quickly dives over the finish line, allowing Chris to start the course.

"Go, Chris," a panting Tracy says while lying on the ground trying to catch her breath.

Chris makes it through the pool and the mud pit with relative ease before climbing the platform for the zip line drop. He quickly makes his way down the platform, zipping down towards the basketball hoop. He makes three shots, shaving another fifteen seconds off of his and Tracy's time. Like Tracy,

Chris struggles up the reverse escalator hill, almost tripping, trying to make his way to the top. He pushes himself to the max, finally makes it up the hill, and quickly runs over, tripping across the finish line much to the others' delight. Tracy, who is still lying on the ground herself, rolls over and faces her exhausted partner.

"Really? You missed two shots? You need to work on your form," Tracy responds, giggling.

"How... how in the hell did you hit all five?" Chris asks, still struggling to breathe.

"All city back in ninety-four and ninety-five," Tracy answers, reaching out her hand to her partner.

They help each other off the ground, still exhausted, waiting for their results. Melissa walks over to interview them.

"Chris, Tracy, that was one hell of a run you put together today," she says. "Do you think it's enough to put you on top?"

"I don't know. I guess we'll see, won't we," Tracy responds, smirking.

"Well, your time has been tallied. We will announce the winner of this season of Team Experiment after these short messages," Melissa says as the camera crew cuts to commercial once more.

Victoria and Sebastian make their way over, showing good sportsmanship congratulating their rivals.

"Shit, this is gonna be close," Sebastian says. "I thought we had it, but I didn't count on Tracy here having skills on the court like that."

"Me neither. Seems my girl's been keeping secrets from me," Victoria teases. "Any other secrets you wanna share?"

Tracy shakes her head, knowing her friend was trying to

find out about the night previous.

"Nothing of note," she replies, with a wink.

Victoria nods her head with approval as the production crew line both teams up with Melissa in the middle. Both teams look a mess with their clothes still stained with mud and are both anxious as the show counts down once more to go live.

"We're back, ladies and gentlemen. It's time to announce the winner of this year's edition of Team Experiment," she says before turning to Victoria and Sebastian. "Guys, you finished your course with a time of six minutes and fifty-four seconds. How do you feel about your time after seeing Tracy and Chris's course time?"

"I feel good about it. I think we're still good," a confident Victoria answers for her team before Melissa turns to Chris and Tracy. "Chris, Tracy, it's the moment of truth. How nervous are you right now?"

"No matter what happens, I can honestly say this show has forever changed me, and I had a blast being here," Chris answers a nodding Melissa. The latter turns her attention towards the camera.

"Okay, it's that time. The time has been tallied. Show us Chris and Tracy's run time," Melissa says as the big TV screen rolls through a few numbers, making everyone anxious.

The number finally generates, showing that Tracy and Chris completed the course at six minutes and forty-nine seconds, just edging out Victoria and Sebastian, who are stunned with the time. Tracy and Chris yell out in excitement as the team hugs each other, knowing they just won the competition.

"Tracy and Chris are the winners!" Melissa exclaims. "They just beat out Victoria and Sebastian by a mere five seconds! One basketball shot away from a tie! Well done, guys! Well done!"

A disappointed Victoria and Sebastian congratulate Tracy and Chris with hugs before making their way into the house to clean up. Tracy and Chris are filled with pure joy after the competition. They struggle not to show any intimate celebrations with each other, settling with fist bumps and side hugs. Melissa claps for them but has something up her sleeve as she approaches.

"Congratulations, you two. You played the game well, and in the end, you took out all your competition. Well done indeed," she says. "However, the game is not over yet."

Chris and Tracy stop in mid-celebration, looking on confused.

"As you know, here on Team Experiment, we're full of twists and turns, and instead of awarding both of you half the money, only one of you will go home with all of the money," Melissa explains, stunning the two friends. "You two will have to decide who takes home the money, and who goes home empty-handed. If you can't agree, there will be one last competition to decide the ultimate winner."

Chris and Tracy are shocked at the new revelation. Chris looks towards Tracy and waves her off. In his mind, one of them will claim the money and split it once they are on the outside. Tracy picks up on his signal and nods her head with approval.

"Now, before you decided, we wanted to give you an insight on your popularity outside of the home," Melissa says with a sinister grin. "You two were the favorite team of all the contestants on the show, and we're here to show you why. Roll the footage."

Tracy and Chris look towards the big screen as clips from the show begin to display showing their interactions with each other. They are laughing at the light-hearted moments until clips of their strategy room sessions started to air. Chris's face drops as Tracy looks on stunned as well. They watch as their most intimate discussions are shown to them, and the world, to see. They don't know how to react as the video clip ends. Melissa looks into the camera with a smile as the fans are shown both Chris and Tracy's reaction to seeing the footage.

"We'll be right back," Melissa says as they go off the air.

"What the fuck is going on?!" Chris exclaims. "Please tell me you didn't broadcast that!"

"Look at your contracts," Melissa says, brushing off the couple's feelings. "All footage shot on the Team Experiment grounds are for us to use as we see fit. It's all perfectly legal."

"Oh my god," Tracy says as she walks off to the lounge area.

An infuriated Chris continues to seek answers from a nonchalant Melissa.

"But… but the strategy room was an off-limits room! How the fuck could you do this to us?!" Chris yells, causing some of the production crew to get concerned.

"Like I said, it was in your contract. If you want to file a complaint, you need to get with the show's producers," Melissa explains, still unconcerned.

"Do you realize what you have done to us?!" Chris replies. "You just ruined our fucking lives!"

"Well, one of you is going home with a million dollars, so I'm sure that will take care of things," Melissa says. "By the way, I only need one of you to announce who's taking home the money. So you should be over there with your friend trying to figure things out."

"Figure things out? Figure things out?!" Chris says before

charging towards Melissa.

He's held back by several crew members as he tries his hardest to get away from their grasps. He's finally pushed over towards the lounge area where Tracy is sitting with her head down in tears. Chris takes a seat as well, trying to calm down and console his friend.

"Tracy, look, I'm-"

"I knew I shouldn't have done this shit. I fucking knew it," she says with a face full of tears. "Oh my god, I can only imagine what they're saying about me. About us."

"It's crazy, I know, but... fuck me. I can't believe this shit. My wife was watching this show. Your husband. Son of a bitch," a frustrated Chris exclaims. "Christ, my son might have even seen it."

Tracy looks towards Chris and can see how upset he is with everything that transpired. While she is devastated herself over the events, she feels even worse for Chris and what this ordeal will put him through. After several moments of silence, she takes a deep breath and grabs her friend's hand.

"Take the money," she says, catching him off guard. "My marriage was already failing. You'll still have a chance to make yours work. A million dollars can make a difference, trust me."

"Take the money? Are you fucking kidding me?" Chris says as if he's offended. "I don't want anything to do with it!"

"Chris, you don't understand. I know you're upset. If you don't want to do it for yourself, do it for your son. You know I'm right," Tracy replies, trying to sell him. "Once we walk out of those gates, you're going to need a bargaining chip."

"And you're not?" Chris questions. "I mean, I know you're not in a good place, but I'm sure James isn't going to want to hear all that shit himself. We can just split it and do it that way if you want."

"No. I don't want it," Tracy quips.

"Well, neither do I," Chris says.

The two friends are at an impasse as neither will budge. Tracy chuckles, which confuses her teammate.

"What's so funny?" Chris asks.

"I'm just… Oh my god, I still can't believe this shit," Tracy says, lowering her head once more. "I mean, I told all my family and friends to watch the show. My mother and my father… oh my god, this is too crazy."

Chris grasps Tracy's hands this time, trying to comfort her as best he can.

"Look at me. I'm not all that close with my family. I'm going to have to deal with my wife, but for the most part, I don't care about how I look in the public eye. Seriously, I want you to take the money. You're going to need it."

Tracy looks into Chris's eyes and can tell that he's not going to take no for an answer. She doesn't want the dirty money either, but it is life-changing that can help her out of a lot of debt she and James have run up. After a few moments, she slowly nods her head with a few tears streaming down her face.

"Okay," she softly says.

"Alright, then it's settled," Chris says as he stands up. "Look, can you take care of the announcement because I might kick that bitch in the head if I see her again?"

Tracy nods her head as she rises as well.

"I'll take care of it," she says as the two embrace one last time.

Chris sighs before looking towards Melissa and frowning.

He's watched by the production staff as he makes his way back into the home while Tracy makes her way over towards Melissa, who greets her with a smile. Tracy isn't in the mood for Melissa and her fake pleasantries.

"Wipe that smile off your fucking face," Tracy says as the countdown to go on air begins. "If I didn't think you'd sue me, I'd slap that wig straight off your bald head ass!"

As the cameras go live, they get a quick glimpse of the fear in Melissa's eyes before she's able to go into her TV personality mode.

"Hello, and we're back," she said nervously. "So Tracy, have you and Chris decided on who's going to take the money?"

"We have," Tracy replies trying her best not to show her anger.

"Well, let America know who is the country's latest millionaire?" Melissa inquires.

Tracy hesitates for a moment as she's having a sudden change of heart. After thinking it through, she takes a deep breath before responding.

"Chris," she says, stunning Melissa. "We decided that Chris will collect the prize money."

"Unbelievable!" Melissa exclaims. "So why did Chris send you out for the announcement?"

"Because Chris didn't want to end up in jail by knocking out a two-faced bitch on national TV," Tracy says, frightening Melissa once more. "Me, I'm a little calmer than my partner, but not by much."

Tracy walks off abruptly, leaving Melissa to close out the show as she tries to calm down.

"That's... well, that's all the time we have for today. I'd

like to once again congratulate Chris Sargent for being this season's winner of Team Experiment! This has truly been one of the most memorable seasons in the show's history. We leave you tonight with some of our favorite clips from the season. Good night, America, and thank you for joining us!" Melissa says to the camera.

As soon as the show signs off, Melissa hurries to collect her things before turning to one of the production assistants.

"Get my car in the driveway! Now!" She exclaims, ready to get out of the house before Tracy or Chris approaches her.

Tracy starts the shower and gets in, with her mind weighing heavy with her thoughts surrounding her and Chris's relationship. As the dirt and grits fall from her body, she thinks back to the night previous where she had him all to herself. While she was happy that the two didn't commit to the sex act, a small part of her still regrets not going all the way with him. Especially since both of their lives are ruined anyway due to the broadcast. The tears on her face are hidden from the water in the shower, but the pain she felt couldn't be hidden. She breaks down, finally submitting to her emotions, and begins sobbing profusely, heartbroken, and filled with guilt.

About an hour has gone by as Chris makes his way out of the front door of the Team Experiment house for the first time in over forty-five days. He's fully dressed, packed, and ready to leave the spotlight behind him. Tracy makes her way out a few moments later with her bag in her hand, and her face filled with sorrow. She's cleaned up and is looking nice, outside of her mood. Chris sighs as he pats her on the shoulder.

"I can't believe you did that," he says, smirking. "Why?"

"Because it was the right thing to do," Tracy replies. "Besides, you deserve better. I might have ruined your marriage, and I didn't set out to-"

"It takes two, Tracy. You didn't ruin anything," Chris points out, trying to remove the burden from his friend. "I can't blame anyone for my choices at this stage in life. I chose you, and to be honest, if I could go back and do it all over, I'd choose you again."

A small smile enters Tracy's face, appreciative of Chris's kind words.

"Thank you. For everything," she says just as their escort pulls up.

Chris nods his head as he helps her with her bags as the two teammates enter the transport. As the car makes its way down the driveway, both Tracy and Chris are lost in their thoughts, wondering what the future holds in their marriage. While stewing over their lives, the two are pleasantly surprised when the main gate to the property opens revealing thousands of fans in support waiting for their departure. Chris and Tracy have developed into iconic status that went viral, and fans from all over have come to see them on their way. The transport struggles to move forward as the crowd blocks their path, restricting much movement.

"I'm sorry about this, sir, ma'am. Security will be through in a minute to clear all this up," the driver says as he waits for support.

Chris and Tracy are stunned looking around the crowd, as they finally realize just how popular the show really is. As security makes their way out and pushes the crowd back, Chris notices his wife is part of the crowd and stops the driver before he pulls off.

"Just a second," he says before quickly exiting the vehicle.

He makes eye contact with his wife as the two see each

other for the first time since the show started.

"Hey, let her through," Chris instructs to security, pointing out his wife. "The woman in red! Yeah, let her through."

Security allows Alexis through the line while pushing everyone else back. Chris doesn't know how his wife will respond after everything that went on during the show. The two look at each other for several moments, not knowing what to do or what to say. With all the chaos going on around them, in their minds, it was just each other. Chris slowly approaches her being careful to not do anything that could potentially set her off, especially with the fans surrounding the area filming with their phones. Tracy watches from the car's back seat, not sure if she should say anything as well. She feels guilty and wanted to apologize to Alexis, but didn't want to make things worse with her presence.

After a brief stare down between Chris and Alexis, their emotions take over as the two walk over and hug each other tightly, much to the crowd's delight. Alexis has tears in her eyes as she hugs her husband tightly with the cheers of the crowd echoing in the background. As Tracy looks at the married couple, a slight smile enters her face, knowing that Chris and his wife will be fine. She takes a deep breath; thankful things didn't get out of hand.

"Let's go," she tells the driver.

"What about Mr. Sargent?" The driver asks.

"Mr. Sargent will be fine," Tracy answers.

The driver nods his head as he slowly makes his way out of the gate and onto the main road. Chris, while still hugging his wife, notices the car pulling off from a distance. He wanted to say things to his teammate before they parted ways for good, but for now, he knew he had a long night ahead of him trying to fix his relationship with his wife.

About an hour later, Tracy finds herself sitting at the airport waiting for her flight. Her husband didn't meet her in Los Angeles like he promised he would. She responded to several texts from family and friends, but nobody was there to meet her. She tried calling James several times, but all the calls went to voicemail. Feeling like an utter failure, Tracy starting checking out the Team Experiment website researching how bad things looked. As she continues to search through her phone, she's startled to see Victoria, who had made her way over to her.

"Hey," Victoria says, approaching with a smile.

"Hey, Vikki. What are you doing here?" Tracy asks.

"Same as you, trying to catch a plane back home," Victoria answers as she takes a seat next to her friend. "My flight was canceled, so apparently, I'm catching a connecting flight back to Houston."

Tracy nods her head as she puts her phone back in her purse. Victoria can see that she's an emotional mess.

"I'm sorry," Victoria says. "I mean, wow. Who would have thought they would have done that. I still can't believe it. If I were you, I'd sue the shit out of that show!"

"It's… it's okay. Honestly, I just want to crawl under a rock and die," Tracy responds. "I don't want to drag this out. I just want out of the spotlight. My husband isn't answering any of my calls; my mom and dad are asking questions. My sister, cousins, and… I'm just so over this. I'm going to be forever remembered as the tramp who almost ruined a good marriage."

"I mean, Chris is to blame too, you know," Victoria points out. "It's not just you."

"Come on, Vikki. You know the double standard we live with," Tracy replies. "He's going to look like the victim in all this once the media spins it. I'm going to be the cheap whore, and life as I know it will end."

Victoria sighs, nodding her head with understanding. After a few moments, a smile slowly grows on her face, as an idea comes to her on how she can help Tracy out.

"You know, it doesn't need to be that way," she says with a smirk.

"What do you mean?" Tracy asks before hearing that her flight is boarding.

"Let's you and me talk on the plane," Victoria responds as she rises. "This may work out in your favor and also open up a wealth of opportunities for both of us."

A suspicious Tracy rises as well as she gathers her things.

"Wealth of opportunity? What are you talking about?" she asks.

Victoria giggles as she leads her friend over to the departure gate going into detail on her plan to fix Tracy's situation. While Tracy isn't fully sold on the idea, her friend did make some valid points for her to think about on the plane ride home.

Chapter 14

Epilogue

In California, in an upscale apartment, Tracy wakes up bright and early and gets prepared to start her day. It's been three years since the events on the show, and a lot has changed in the former contestant's life. She's become a reality icon, along with her roommate Victoria, thanks to taking advantage of the show's fame. Victoria's plan was simple, jump ahead of the stories, and use her fame for interviews and other opportunities. Tracy hesitated initially to fit into her normal life the first month back in Houston but realized she could never return to that mold with everything the show revealed about her. She couldn't even walk into a grocery store without people recognizing her and wanting to take a picture. She decided to take Victoria up on her idea as the two started touring the circuit doing interviews and appearances all over. She has since been on several other reality shows and is one of the biggest draws in the genre. It's not what she planned for her life, but it not only made her famous, it made her financially stable.

She's in the mirror checking herself out making sure her outfit was fitting her perfectly, when her doorbell rings. She walks over to answer her door passing through her luxurious apartment, decked out with high-end appliances and artwork that gives the place a modern look. She's stunned when she opens the door for Chris, who she hasn't seen in person since that faithful day on the final episode. She's speechless as Chris can tell she's shocked to see him. Both are stunned as Chris looks at his now glamourous friend, and Tracy looks at Chris's fully formed beard.

"Hey," he says, still a little nervous about seeing her after all this time.

"Hey," she timidly responds.

"You... well, I'm going to be honest, you're harder to track down than the Taliban," Chris jokes, hoping to bring some levity to the conversation.

"I... um... yeah. I'm, well... what are you doing here?" She asks, stuttering her way through the shock.

"I was in the neighborhood, and thought I'd stop by," Chris responds with a smile. "Are you going to ask me in?"

"Oh, shit, I'm sorry. Yes, please, come in," Tracy says as she stands to the side.

Chris walks into the apartment and is blown away with the setup. Tracy closes the door behind him, as Chris nods his head with approval.

"Well, this is exceptionally nice," he says looking around the apartment. "I guess you made out pretty well."

"Well, it's not just mine. Vikki stays here too," Tracy points out. "She's been out the last few weeks on the Big Brother show. I don't know if you keep up with it or not, but she's been doing pretty good for herself as well."

"Yeah, I took a hiatus on the reality shows after our experience," Chris admits. "I checked you out on a show or two briefly, but couldn't get into it like I used to for the most part."

Tracy nods her head as she walks into the kitchen and fixes her a glass of water.

"Can I get you something? Juice, or a Coke?" She offers.

"No, I'm good," Chris says as he takes a seat at the kitchen island.

Both he and Tracy look at each other, still stunned to be in the same room together.

"So, how's Anthony and Alexis doing?" Tracy asks, breaking the awkward silence.

"Anthony's doing fine. They both are actually. He's growing up so fast. Just turned eleven last month," Chris answers.

"Almost those teen years," Tracy replies, smirking. "Sooner or later, he's going to hate your guts. I hope you're ready for that."

"Well, I think his mother hates my guts more than he ever will," Chris reveals.

"Oh my god, what happened?"

Chris sighs before going into his story.

"After the show, things never were the same again," Chris explains. "She wanted to forgive me, she really did, but she could never get over what I said. She wasn't even that mad about the sex. It's the fact that I told you that I loved you that shook her. She couldn't get over that, and because of that, we divorced six months after. I guess she felt more betrayed by my words than anything. I don't blame her. I deserved everything I got."

Tracy looks towards her friend feeling guilty in her part with breaking up this marriage.

"I'm so sorry, Chris," she says. "I wish I could go back and fix it."

"It's not your fault," Chris responds. "The way things were going, it was bound to happen anyway. We just weren't a fit for each other. We got married for Anthony, and it just didn't work out."

Tracy nods her head before taking a sip of her water.

"I heard you and James divorced soon after too," Chris says.

"Yeah. Turns out that I wasn't the only one who had an affair," Tracy admits. "His ass was sleeping around with any and everybody. Even in my own bed, which I couldn't believe. Sex is one thing, but to bring it into my home was another. He had the nerve to check me about my one-time infidelity when he was running around town with multiple women. It was probably a month after the show ended when we split. He still calls me now and then, trying to make up with me. I just think he wants a piece of the pie now that I have a little cash to my name."

"Damn. Sorry to hear that," Chris responds. "I knew you were having issues and all, but I didn't know it was like that."

"Yeah, well, what can you do, I guess," Tracy says as she makes her way on the other side of the island, taking a seat next to Chris. "So, now that we're caught up, why don't you tell me the real reason you're here."

"Like, I said, I was in the neighborhood, and figured I'd give you a look," Chris responds to an unconvinced Tracy.

"So you just happen to be in L.A.?" Tracy quips, smirking. "I mean, it's not like it's a quick drive to Dallas or anything."

Chris laughs as he nods his head. He knew Tracy wouldn't go for a generic answer he's given her.

"Okay, I'll be honest, I've probably been looking for you

for the past four months," Chris admits. "I checked websites, social media, basically everything I could trying to find you. I was about to give up when some guy in Chinatown sold me a map of stars for ten bucks."

"So, wait a minute? My address is on a map of the stars?" A confused Tracy asks. "I don't know if I should be pissed or flattered for being considered a star. But forget all that for the moment. You've been looking for me for four months? Why?"

"You know why," Chris replies. "Well at this stage, I hope you know why."

Tracy sighs as she did know what Chris wanted from her. She wasn't certain, however, that she wanted the same thing.

"So you show up at my door three years later like 'hey, I'm here, and I want to pick up where we left off all those years ago'?" She questions. "I mean, what if I was married or something. I could have been dating someone who was staying with me. Did you ever consider that?"

"I did. The Chinaman who sold me the map told me you were single though, so I felt confident about my approach," Chris fires back.

"How in the hell does this Chinaman know so much about my life?" A confused Tracy asks. "I might need to get in touch with my lawyer or something cause this is too much."

"Leave the Chinaman be," Chris says with a smile. "If it wasn't for him, I wouldn't be here now sitting with the one woman I've always loved. If anything, I got off cheap."

A grinning Tracy shakes her head, still in disbelief.

"Chris, that was a long time ago," Tracy says. "I've changed. I'm sure you've changed. It may not be a good time for all of that. What you're asking me here is... I don't know, almost stalkerish if we're being real."

"Ah, I get it. Get a little fame, and it's down with the little people," Chris jokes, causing Tracy to burst into laughter.

"That's not at all what I'm saying," she replies.

"Then what's the issue? The last couple of times we were together, we both were married. Now that we're both available, it's the wrong time?" Chris asks as if he's confused. "This may actually be the best time we've ever had."

"Yeah, but I don't want to be that girl that gets looked at side-eyed," Tracy points out. "I mean, what if me and Alexis meet at an event or something? How's that going to look?"

"She got married almost a year and a half ago," Chris points out. "She's over you, trust me. Even if she wasn't, so what! I'm the one who isn't over you, and I can honestly say I don't know if I ever will be over you. What do I need to do to convince you otherwise? Do I need to get tips from the Chinaman, or what?"

Tracy giggles for the moment as she looks at a desperate Chris begging her for a chance to be together. She's still skeptical after all this time. She thought she had put him behind her, but just like when she saw him for the first time at the Team Experiment House, it brought back all kinds of feelings she thought were long gone. Chris is waiting for a response from Tracy who continues to go back and forth with it in her mind.

"Well?" Chris responds impatiently. "Are we going to do this right, or what?"

"I don't know," Tracy replies. "I mean, you did cheat on your last wife, so how do I know I can trust you?"

Chris looks at Tracy strangely before the two friends burst into laughter.

"That's... that's good. That's real funny," Chris sarcastically responds.

"The look on your face was priceless," Tracy says in mid-laugh. "Seriously though, Chris, I don't know. I mean, like I said, I'm not the same woman I was back then. There's a lot about me you might not like. Especially since I'm now apparently on the map of stars. I'm a known face, and everywhere we go, there would be paparazzi looking to get a picture of us to write a story, basically calling me a homewrecker and you a cheat. Are you really ready to be the buzz of every social media outlet?"

"You already know the answer to that," Chris replies, smirking. "What else you got?"

"I don't think you are thinking clearly here. The show almost ruined us. You went into hiding after it was all said and done. I went out and faced it. These tabloid folks, the magazines, and the social media folks are ruthless, and they're going to rip up to shreds after they see us... aw the hell with it," Tracy says before catching Chris off guard and kissing him, proving that the feelings he felt for her were mutual.

The two continue to kiss each other, longing for this feeling for years. Just as Chris is about to undress her, Tracy stops him.

"What?" He asks.

"You never did give me my half of the money, you know that right?" Tracy says, grinning.

"I tried to give you all the money, remember?" Chris points out. "You're the one that gave it away. It doesn't matter anyway cause Alexis took it all."

"Oh, hell no. Last time I checked, it's half and half," Tracy fires back.

"Do you know how much taxes they took from that? Not to mention we were taxed the following year for earned income as well. They don't tell you that when you win that type of money," Chris replies. "What little money we did have, she took it in the divorce."

"So what you're telling me is that you were seeking me out just to live off me, is that it?" Tracy jokes. "What the hell do I need you for then? You're useless."

"You wasn't saying I was useless back at the cell shop," Chris reminds her.

The two continue to go back and forth with each other, laughing and joking before making their way into the living room. The room goes silent as Chris becomes the aggressor this time around and lifts Tracy off her feet, lying her on the couch. He begins kissing her once again as both he and Tracy finally are able to get what they've been longing for. A little over five years after their affair, the two are connected to each other for the first time, and look to continue their connection for years to come.

Check out more great E. Nigma readings at:

www.enigmakidd.com

To submit a manuscript to be considered,
email us at
submissions@majorkeypublishing.com

Be sure to LIKE our Major Key Publishing
page on Facebook!

Made in the USA
Monee, IL
10 November 2020